GALACTIC SALESMAN TRILOGY
SYNOPSIS

a Summary and Synopsis of the
3 Science Fiction Novels:

1) Mission of the Galactic Salesman
2) Mission Beyond the Ice Cave:
   Atlantis-Mexico-Zotola
3) Heritage Findings from Atlantis

written by
Robert S. Sanders, Jr.
© 1995-2000

GALACTIC SALESMAN TRILOGY SYNOPSIS

use of the words and concepts of:
Danetar, Delikadove, Dolphs, Shakeilar
by permission of Martin A. Enticknap and via his novel:
EXODUS: the Dolph/in Saga, ISBN: 1-928798-35-7
dream of a galactic salesman and crystal ball idea provided by:
Martin A. Enticknap, 1994 among other
helpful ideas, concepts, conversations, explanations and analyses

cover design by: Brian Matthews
Jobsoft Design and Development Inc.
Murfreesboro, Tennessee

selected drawings by contributing artists:
1)Jason Daniel Fisher, 2)David DuBois, 3)Mark J. Volzer

Library of Congress Control Number: 2003093941

ISBN: 1-928798-10-1

type: science fiction-adventure

Armstrong Valley Publishing Company
P.O. Box 1275
Murfreesboro, TN 37133-1275
ph: 615-895-5445
Fax: 615-893-2688

printed in the United States of America

Welcome to the galactic salesman science fiction trilogy, a great set of novels with fun and wholesome adventure, which promote peace, travel, friendship and communication, NOT galactic wars and battles, like so many other science fiction novels.

It all begins when a galactic salesman has a mission to link Earth's telephone network with his home star system and other star systems, as well. His real name is Tomarius (Tom), and he makes a deal with a group of teenagers, Robert Joslin and his friends, grants them the gift of transport by thought, and together they build a galactic communications device in the corner of the Joslin's woods on their farm in Tennessee.

Robert and his friends enjoy numerous adventures. With their gift of transport, they travel far and wide to many places, including other star systems.

In the sequel, they meet some lively young fellows: Rinto, Fraxino, and Chispo. They are descendants from Atlantis and are living in the Orion star system. Robert and his friends go home with them and spend a lot of time there, and together they help Tom, the galactic salesman with another mission, to go to the mountains of northern Mexico and clear a mysterious communications block between Earth and the Orion system.

All of this is just a practice run for the grandest project of them all, a major galactic station involving millions of Earth's telephone numbers, to be built high up in the mountains of northern Alaska. During the project, they unearth five bronze crates, each containing a time frozen body . . . from Atlantis!

They revive them. Discover what information and insights the Atlanteans have to offer.

Join Robert and his friends on their travels, and venture with them as they help Tom and his crew in building the galactic station in Alaska, what it features, from adventures, to time travel, and how it . . .

Note: This is a Summary and Synopsis, which is approximately 10% the size of the full length novels.

The Flowering Sun Tree

(Liriodendron chinense, Liriodendron tulipfera)

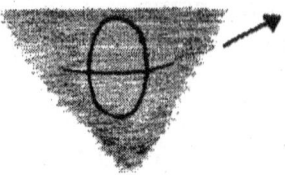

Each flower holds a sunshine in its cup
The yellow sun gives forth
Through its orange flames
To the green of life . . . the **forest**
A sacred story this was
To early modern humans.

They brought with them from Lyra
That piece of heritage, that knowledge
So sacred to their race
When they colonized Earth
1.6 million years ago.

A reminder of their home world
A tree of great size
Of superior characteristics
Fast growing and long lived
Its leaf growth pattern so unique
There is no comparison.

The sacred Flowering Sun Tree
Of Lyran origin it came
For a new beginning
For a new life
To a new world . . . **Earth**.

written by Robert S. Sanders, Jr.
May 2000

Summary and Synopsis of:
MISSION OF THE GALACTIC SALESMAN
written by: Robert S. Sanders, Jr., 1995

How can meeting a galactic salesman alter the summer plans of some teenagers?

Introduction and Character Sketch

This story takes place in 1985 in Middle Tennessee and is mainly about a group of eight teenage fellows who are in their junior year in high school. They are all great friends of one another, are morally straight, open-minded, smart, enthusiastic, and interesting. All of them have a real quest for adventure, exploration, and travel.

The main character is Robert Joslin who lives on a farm southwest of Murfreesboro. The story opens in the winter with Robert and some of his friends sledding down the slopes of a nearby hill. Later, there is a visit to the high school where they attend. One March weekend they all meet on Robert's farm to camp out and make plans for a summer road trip and hiking adventure.

Robert has an amazing dream that night of being able to travel to other planets in other star systems, and when he wakes up, he realizes that he has retained this ability in real life. He is able to pass this ability on to his friends, and they alter their plans and have a great summer adventure travelling to and from places on Earth and other planets. They learn many things about the galaxy and about life on other planets and also learn about some of the past history of Earth and how it came to be. Through their experiences, they come to realize that they know many things that few, if any people on Earth know.

Robert has lived on his parents' farm all of his life, and his father, Bob, is a full-time farmer of crops and cattle along with being a part-time lobbyist. His mother, Pat, is a former school teacher. Robert has a keen interest in travelling and exploring, bicycling, plantlife, and the sciences. He grew up being a believer in conventional evolution of life on Earth and leaned toward believing only what there was convincing evidence for. However, his mind became more open to new ideas, and he's always listened to what others have to say. During their adventures, he and his friends learn a lot and alter their belief systems accordingly.

Chris Chanford is interested in philosophy and lives in the south part of Murfreesboro. He and Robert have known each other since 7th grade, and he sometimes helps the others in understanding the philosophies and differences in the foreign cultures of the civilizations that they visit.

Morris England is a very intuitive person, to say the least, even though he doesn't like to call himself psychic, and he lives a few miles east of Murfreesboro. He is able to sense many answers and explanations from the spirit world, both in dreams and in real life. Through his intuitive abilities, he carries a great deal of

1

knowledge about Earth and other star systems. Like Chris, he understands and explains the philosophies about the reasons that people and things are the way that they are.

On the same night that Robert has his dream, Morris also has a dream in which he meets Tom, who is both a galactic salesman and a communications engineer from the planet around Sirius B in the Sirius binary star system. Tom informs Morris that the Sirians have lost contact with their fellow Sirians now residing on Earth as human beings and proposes his mission to have Robert and his friends build a galactic communications device to link Earth's telephone network to them and also to other star systems. In the dream, he makes a deal with Morris. Can Tom fulfill his mission and re-establish contact with their fellow Earth-incarnated Sirians?

William Johns is a friend and distant cousin of Robert, and he lives near Rockvale, which is five miles from Robert's place. He has an interest in old cars and, like Robert, is a firm believer in only the basics when it comes to cars. He is the primary helper on Robert's car project at the beginning of the story.

William's father works for the phone company and knows a lot about telephone equipment. He is very essential in helping them build the required switching equipment for use in the galactic communications device and is able to obtain surplus central office equipment for that purpose.

Steven Price is a good friend of Robert's, having known him since middle school, and he has lived in the southeast of Murfreesboro all of his life. His parents are teachers. Steven also has an interest in old cars but is more interested in auto body than mechanics, and he owns an immaculate 6-cylinder 3-speed Chevrolet Bel Air. In addition to his interest in cars, he also loves to tinker with electronic circuitry and proves very useful in modifying some of the electronic components used in the galactic communications device that they build.

Steven at first hesitates about travelling and having adventures, but soon comes to love it as he has a taste of it. As a result of his participation in their adventures and also in the construction of the galactic communications device, he comes to realize how important communication is and how it far exceeds and surpasses useless weaponry and war.

Andrew Tremain moved into Tennessee in 1979. His parents are missionaries, and as a result of that, he has lived in other parts of the world. Andrew lives in Murfreesboro and is very knowledgeable on the transmission and reception of communications equipment. He is always interested in what is happening and has some helpful suggestions in the method of construction of the sending-receiving towers that are built in conjunction with the galactic communications device.

James Westfield is new to Tennessee, having moved from Devonport, Tasmania, Australia in December 1984. His father is a builder and is as strong as an ox, and they live on a farm around six miles east of Robert's place. They quickly become great friends since both of them have a real interest in plantlife and travel. James is very straightforward or concrete as far as not believing in anything psychic or paranormal. In addition to passing on his knowledge of Australian plantlife to the others, he has a burning desire to travel and experiences enough surprises during their adventures to really astound him.

Paul Wilson is an old-time friend of Robert's, having known him since early childhood. He has lived near Murfreesboro all of his life, and his father runs an aluminum fabrication plant making mostly utility boxes. Paul has a keen sense of business and is musically talented and enjoys the outdoor adventures of their summer travels.

Greg Nelson and Eric Smotherman are two more friends who do not participate in the whole adventure because of their busy schedules. Greg eventually wants to be a dentist, and Eric wants to work in the pottery business, which is what his father does. Both of them live in Murfreesboro.

There are additional characters.

Mr. Gordon Mayfield is their high school science teacher, and he is interested in extraterrestrial life. His discussions in class contribute somewhat to Robert's having his amazing dream.

Mr. Michael Vance is their American history professor and causes the class to have original thoughts and to speculate and give their opinions on certain events and alternative scenarios.

Read through the adventures of Robert and his friends as they help fulfill Tom's mission, travel to many places, including other star systems, and meet alien lifeforms, both male and female.

Chapter 1: THE MEETING OF THE SIRIAN COUNCIL

The story opens in late January, 1985 on a snowy day in the middle of winter with Robert Joslin, William Johns, and Morris England sledding down the Pinnacle of the Versailles Hills fifteen miles southwest of Murfreesboro, Tennessee. They have a great time racing each other several times down the steep slope of the hill. They comment on how cold the weather has been.

After several descents, they decide to walk to the summit to see the view of the snow-covered countryside. On their way up, Robert and William talk about Robert's recently purchased 1979 Ford LTD station wagon, and he tells William that he's going to put a 6-cylinder 4-speed in it. They make plans to work on it together the next month when the snow clears and the weather is warmer.

When they reach the summit, they comment on the scenery. Suddenly, Morris has a strange feeling and tells the others that some strange thoughts are going through his head. Robert and William immediately become interested in what Morris is experiencing and listen intently while Morris describes that he gets the feeling that a group of people in another star system are meeting at that present moment to have a discussion about the people of Earth. It seems that they need around 10 people to help them on a project of some sort, something about the fact that they have lost contact with some of their people on Earth. He hears something about travel by thought, whatever that means, and he loses telepathic contact.

Robert and William are somewhat astounded and ask Morris what that was all about. He explains that it is similar to a person's ear ringing, but he also hears faint messages at times. As the ringing fades after a minute, so do the faint messages. They speculate that Morris has mental telepathy. Morris admits that could be what it is.

*   *   *

The scene changes and is now on planet Sirius B in the Sirius star system over 8 light years away. It is a warm sunny day on this mostly dry planet of Cypress-Pine shrubs and Cactus plants, and the Sirian Council is having a meeting outdoors. Twelve members gather to discuss the problem they are having with their people who have gone on to be incarnated as human beings on Earth in the Sol System. Basically, they have lost contact with them because they are not fully conscious beings like the Sirians are.

They discuss a possible solution, and Tom, a galactic salesman and engineer, comes forth with the possibility of tapping into Earth's telephone network, pointing out that nearly every resident of Earth has a telephone. Wasser, the leader of the council, expresses his approval, and the council decides to find a group of teenagers who are very intelligent to help Tom with the project.

Caymar, another member of the council, suggests to Tom that he offer his quartz crystal ball to one of the members of the group, and Wasser suggests that Tom grant the gift of transport by thought to every one of the teenagers who help

4

him. Tom agrees to the suggestions and tells the council that he will meet with his crew, make plans, and draw up a proposal.

Chapter 2: THE CAR PROJECT

A month has passed, and it is a nice warm sunny day in late February, 1985. Robert Joslin and his friend and distant cousin, William Johns have been working on Robert's 1979 Ford LTD station wagon. They had spent several afternoons at Robert's place working on it, and they had successfully installed the 6-cylinder motor out of a 1969 Ford Econoline van and the 3 O/D (4-speed) manual transmission out of a 1980 Ford F-100 pickup truck. Today, they are figuring out how to mount the clutch linkage. After several hours of working on it this afternoon, they realize that it's getting dark, and they go inside the Joslin's house to eat supper with Robert's parents.

While they are eating supper, Robert's father discusses how big the job is that Robert and William are working on. He also asks Robert's reassurance that he will also do some farm chores including some fence cleaning. Robert tells him not to worry, that he will get to it.

Robert and William begin talking about what they are going to do this summer, and they conceive the idea of taking a big road trip out West with the modified Ford station wagon. They think it's such a great idea that they phone eight other friends to see if they want to go, and all except two of them say yes, that they can come.

Next, they are at Riverdale High School in southwest Murfreesboro, Tennessee, and the first scene is in U.S. history class with Mr. Michael Vance as the teacher. The day is Wednesday, February 27, and Mr. Vance decides to discuss possible alternative scenarios to World War I in consideration of what would have happened if the Germans had won. Several in the class give their ideas.

James Westfield presents his theory based on an Australian viewpoint, and Morris England gives his far-out and far-fetched viewpoint based on his highly intuitive abilities.

The discussion shifts to their viewpoint on the issue of war in general. A student whose last name is Tomlin boasts about the fame and glory of war. Steven Price points out that we wouldn't be here if it hadn't been for our forefathers' fighting and bloodshed. Robert Joslin points out that a person in England has just as many freedoms there as does an American here. Morris England really gets into it and brings in some far-fetched ideas from other star systems, and James Westfield finishes off the class discussion by pointing out how white Australian settlers wiped out every Aborigine from the state of Tasmania!

The seven-second beep sounds, and they go on to chemistry class with Mr. Gordon Mayfield. He is an interesting science teacher who, every few weeks, gets off the subject and discusses the possibility of extraterrestrials and UFO's. Today

5

is one of those lucky days, and he tells the class about a couple of his own sightings. They theorize on their possibility and discuss what method of travel the UFO's could use.

During the discussion, it dawns on Robert for the first time that quite possibly, beings from other star systems could have visited Earth and brought life here and could have taken life from here to elsewhere. He brings up the subject to Mr. Mayfield and gets his opinion.

After chemistry class, James walks up to Robert and comments that Mr. Mayfield brought up some off-the-wall stuff and asks him if Mayfield is on something. Robert reassures James that Mr. Mayfield is one of the straightest people he will ever meet, and also says that he enjoys it when he gets off the subject like today.

After school, Robert goes home and works on his car and and later phones William and tells him that he has successfully installed the clutch linkage. The rest of the week at school goes fine, and on Saturday, March 2, William comes out to Robert's place and they wire up the wiring harness and get the car running. Steven comes over later in the afternoon and comments on how well the project is going. The three of them take it for a drive for the first time. They discover some more problems which they will work on another day.

When they return after their short drive, their other friends arrive.

Chapter 3: THE AMAZING DREAM

Chris, Morris, Andrew, James, and Paul arrive, and they decide to camp in the Joslin's woods for the night. That evening, they get to talking about extraterrestrial matters and Morris tells them about some of his dreams and insists to the others that there's definitely life out there on other star systems. Paul agrees that it would be arrogant to think that Earth was the only planet in the universe with life on it. Robert relates to the others about his dream about going to Mars when he was age 12, and William comments that he wishes he could also have dreams like that.

Then Morris tell them about his dream of being out on another planet and of a galactic salesman who offered him a quartz crystal ball, telling him that he would have to buy it. He tells them how this galactic salesman went on and on about the ball, telling him all the details and showing it to him. Morris says he told the salesman he had had enough of hearing about this bloomin' ball and told him he was going to wake up on him, and he did. The other fellows are really intrigued and comment on how interesting his dream was.

Steven goes on to tell them that he believes in reincarnation and proceeds to tell Robert that they were brothers in Russia in the 1700's and that travel was forbidden and that Robert swore that if he ever lived another lifetime on Earth that he would travel as much as possible. Robert informs Steven that he just doesn't have any past life memories. Chris comments that he needs some proof on case studies before he would believe in reincarnation.

All of this discussion must have gone to Robert's head because that night he has an amazing dream of being with his friends on another planet. They had the ability to travel by thought. All they had to do was to place their hands on either side of themselves, think a certain way, and a pink glow would overcome them along with the sound of whirring wind. They would dematerialize and rematerialize to the location to which they would think themselves. They transported themselves to several places, and they transported objects, as well. Robert transported himself home and waited for the others, but they didn't come.

He soon wakes up and is astounded at what he has just dreamed. It is just getting light outside. Morris gets up, comes over to Robert and motions him to come outside and talk with him.

Once outside, Morris relates to him about a dream he had, and quite to Robert's surprise, it was the very same dream he had! Morris explains that his dream went further, and the same galactic salesman came and offered that same quartz crystal ball to him again. Morris told him he wasn't very interested in having it, and he explains that the galactic salesman offered Morris and his friends the gift of transport by thought and also the gift of transmitting visual images to Morris, in addition to the crystal ball, if all of them would help him build a galactic communications device to link Earth's telephone network to his home planet and to other star systems, as well. In the dream, Morris agreed and made a deal with him.

They decide to inform the others. Robert does the explaining and tells them they now have the ability to travel by thought. Immediately, they use their new gift, and to get used to it, they transport to Tasmania and, quite to their astonishment, arrive in the middle of a Buttongrass plain dotted with occasional Pencil Pines. James explains about the scenery, and minutes later they return to the Joslin's woods.

Once back home, they walk down to the Joslin's house and have breakfast. Robert picks up the phone to call Greg and Eric who could not come over this weekend and is very surprised to discover that the ringback tone of Murfreesboro's phone numbers has changed to sound just like Nashville's! He thinks he dialled the number wrong, immediately hangs up, and redials the number. Then he calls a number in Eagleville and discovers it has also changed! Robert tells the others, and William, whose father works for the phone company, informs Robert that Murfreesboro which was on crossbar, and Eagleville which was on step-by-step, got new phone exchanges last night. They are now on digital.

They ponder this fact, and come up with an idea that some of the old phone equipment, the step-by-step equipment in Eagleville, may be very useful for building the telephone exchange required to link Earth's telephone network to other star systems. William phones his father, and he invites everyone over to Eagleville to tour the step office. They are off to Eagleville!

Chapter 4: THE TOUR OF THE STEP OFFICE

Eagleville was a small crossroads of a town 20 miles southwest of Murfreesboro, and it had around 400 people. The road going to it was State Highway 99, a narrow winding road with plenty of curves, humps, and dips. It had no shoulders, and the short bridges crossing creeks were never wider than they had to be, barely wide enough to allow two trucks to squeeze by each other, short of clashing their mirrors. Closer to Eagleville, there were, in actual fact, places on the highway that contained a bridge on a hump on a curve.

Once in Eagleville, they pull over to the roadside, and Mr. Johns greets them and gives them a full tour of the telephone exchange, telling them exactly how a step-by-step exchange works. They are fascinated. While he is giving them a tour, Mr. Johns discovers a clear quartz crystal ball sitting on some of the batteries, and he comments that he doesn't remember seeing that before. Morris perks up and comes over and exclaims that it is just like the one in the dream! With that said, Mr. Johns gives it to him. Morris is overjoyed and just stares at it, astounded beyond belief.

They break the news of their plans with a galactic salesman to build a phone exchange in the corner of the Joslin's woods, and Mr. Johns is at first surprised and then becomes so curious that he offers to help with the entire project. They are pleased that this has worked out so well. Mr. Johns takes them out of the building, locks up, and they go home. He agrees to bring over much of the equipment when the tearout would begin tomorrow.

Robert, William, and Morris go up to the corner of the Joslin's woods and speculate on the exact location of the communications device and make plans to clear a space for the building and how they are going to build it. They make plans to have each one of them chip in $100 to pay for the building materials. After making these plans, Robert and Morris decide to break the news to the Joslins.

The next day in the afternoon after school, Mr. Johns arrives with a truck and trailer full of the step office equipment. He and Robert unload all of it, switches, boxes, racks and all, into the Joslin's tenant house, no longer lived in. Next, they make plans on how they are going to have it wired up to connect it to Murfreesboro. He agrees to bring his backhoe later in the week to dig a ditch for the wires.

On Wednesday, March 6, Robert, William, and Steven are working on Robert's Ford LTD wagon, swapping out the 2.26 ratio rear end for a 3.55. They make comments about the car, and Steven compliments the exhaust system installed by the local muffler shop. They take it for another test drive and realize the car is now road worthy. Robert is relieved to have his car project completed.

During the afternoon, they clear the site for the building in the corner of the Joslin's woods. Mr. Johns will come Sunday with his backhoe.

Chapter 5: THE TRIP TO SAVAGE GULF

It is Saturday, March 9, and all of them have decided to take a weekend backpacking trip to Savage Gulf State Natural Area. All of them meet at the Joslins, and they take two of their cars from there. James, Morris, and William ride with Robert in his LTD wagon. The others ride with Paul.

As they drive to Savage Gulf via Woodbury and McMinnville, Robert and the three others talk about cars, and James informs them about some of the cars of Australia and how they compare to American models. He also reminds them that they drive on the left in Australia.

Next, Robert tells James that the McMinnville area is well known for its nurseries, and James says he and his father will have to return there for some trees. Also, Robert tells James more about Savage Gulf.

From McMinnville, they drive on the highway to Beersheba Springs and turn left to go to the Stone Door entrance. They park, obtain overnight permits, and take off hiking through the canyon after descending through Stone Door.

Robert informs them about the types of trees growing in this area, and all of them discuss the effects of acid rain and environmental damage in the Appalachian Mountains east of there.

After hiking for several miles through the canyon, they arrive at Savage Creek, turn right, and ascend alongside the creek into a virgin forest of Oaks, Hickories, Poplars, Hemlocks, and other trees, some as large as 6 feet in diameter and others having no limbs until 75 feet up the trunk. All of them exclaim how impressed they are at the unusual size of the trees in this area. The terrain is rough going, but it's worth it to them to see this virgin forest.

Finally, they arrive at a nice site considerably up from Savage Creek and set up camp. They explore the area until dark, eat supper, and then ask Morris about his ability to transmit visual images. He proceeds to tell them, and he transmits to them a mountain scene from a planet in another galaxy. He tells them there's a stone hut near the top of the mountain and that there is a psychic woman up there who gives readings.

Everyone decides to transport there by thought, and they successfully arrive to a mountainous slope with beautiful alpine meadows and coniferous trees. They climb the mountain, find the stone hut on a grassy knoll near the top, and sure enough, just like Morris told them, they find the psychic woman at home. She's pleased to meet them, introduces herself as Virginia, tells them she is a woman from Earth who takes her vacations here, and gives them astounding readings. They are actually impressed with her abilities and accuracy. She informs them that the name of the planet they are on is called Lopeia. She also informs Morris that his newly acquired crystal ball is very important to him in his life.

She states that travelling is a fantastic way to to learn about the diversity of life and how all types are important, how they have their place in the world, and how they all need to be cared for, and she wishes them a great time on their future travels.

When she finishes her readings, they climb to the summit and view the fantastic sunset and from there, transport back to their campsite in the Savage Creek gorge and camp for the night.

The next morning, they all make comments, still impressed at how Virginia gave such accurate readings. Morris gives his theory that her spirit guides communicate with the guides of whomever she is talking to, and that is probably how she gets her answers.

They hike further up the gorge and see more big trees and come upon the largest tree in this gorge, a Buckeye tree 6 feet in diameter. Robert is very surprised that it is a Buckeye tree instead of a Poplar or a Hemlock.

Next, they turn around and walk all the way out but get caught in a violent thunderstorm for 20 minutes and take shelter under some overhanging rocks alongside a creek. After the storm, they walk the rest of the way out, climb up Stone Door, and return to their cars.

They drive home. Robert tells his parents about their adventures and then goes to the woods to inspect Mr. Johns' backhoe work. He has done a fine job. A concrete truck will come later in the week to pour the floor for the building.

Chapter 6: THE GALACTIC COMMUNICATIONS DEVICE

Monday afternoon after school, Robert and Morris meet and go around town to gather supplies and building materials for the building. They order the concrete blocks, lumber, and roofing materials and give directions to deliver them to the site later.

The next day, Robert and William meet after school and build the forms for the concrete floor to be poured, after which the concrete truck arrives and pours the pad.

On Saturday, March 16, they all meet and literally build the entire 16' by 20' building in one day, and on Sunday, Mr. Johns arrives with a phone company van and helps them install the step office. They bolt the racks to the floor and hang the Strowger switches on the shelves in the same manner as they were in Eagleville. After lots of soldering to reassemble the step office, Mr. Johns finally triumphs that it is complete. It was wired with one to one trunking and contains 20 lines.

Suddenly, Morris gets a strange feeling, and the galactic salesman suddenly appears and startles everyone. He's teleported down from Sirius B and introduces himself as Tom. He proceeds to explain the problem the Sirians are having in communicating with their people who now reside on Earth as human beings. He explains that Earth humans used to be fully conscious like the Sirians still are, but some of their genetics were disconnected by the Atlanteans during unscrupulous experiments they conducted.

Mr. Johns shows Tom the newly installed step office, and Tom is seriously impressed with the electro-mechanical hardware of the Strowger switches and with their durability. He gives his approval and informs Mr. Johns of the plans that he and his crew have with the installation of the receiver/sender towers and how they are to be connected to the step office. The towers are to use huge metal electro-magnetic rings 8 feet in diameter, each with a pyramidal-shaped crystal 2 feet tall in its center. Gravity waves will be used for the transmitting and receiving because gravity waves are almost instantaneous in comparison to electro-magnetic waves. He and Mr. Johns come up with a solution for connecting them along with the input and suggestions of Robert, Andrew, and Steven. They realize they still need more materials to make it work. With that planned, Tom teleports back home to Sirius B.

On Tuesday, March 19, the phone company arrives and hangs the ten-line trunk cable to connect the exchange to Murfreesboro. Mr. Johns obtains a battery bank from surplus phone equipment and also obtains surplus car telephone equipment.

Saturday, March 23 arrives. The weather is nice, and all of Robert's friends arrive. Mr. Mayfield also arrives, as he wants to see the events and meet Tom, the galactic salesman. They install the rest of the required equipment to enable them to connect the step office to the receiver/transmitter towers.

Later that morning, Tom arrives with his crew, and 5 receiver/transmitter towers each 15 feet tall, suddenly appear in the Joslin's barnyard. Next, they levitate them over to the site in the corner of the woods and firmly anchor them to the outcropping limestone rocks behind the building. Each tower has an electro-magnetic ring and crystal apparatus, complete with servo motors to rotate them in several directions. Tom further directs the crew as they proceed to wire the towers into the step office. A solar panel and battery bank is installed to supply power to the towers.

Tom next realizes that they need telephones to install at their extraterrestrial telephone stations, and Robert takes him down to his house and shows him their Western Electric black rotary dial desk phone with a black metal dial. Tom is impressed with the phone's durability and takes it to the barnyard and has his crew duplicate it by levitating it and moving it horizontally and sending it back briefly in time once a second to cause a duplicate to appear next to it. 120 physical copies are made of the Joslin's telephone, and Tom gives the original one back to Robert. Everyone is very impressed at this seemingly magical feat, especially when they suddenly disappear as they are teleported away to Sirius B for storage.

Tom talks with them for a while and explains why gravity waves travel far faster than the speed of light, seeing that gravity waves are non-physical and are just a distortion of the time-frame network. He explains why he chose Robert and his friends and also compliments all of them on a job well done in building the galactic communications device.

Mr. Johns now assigns phone numbers to the star systems, and Tom now telepathically directs his additional crew on Sirius B to connect one of the telephones to the telephone station there and to dial this step office. A few minutes later, the telephone inside the step office building rings, and Tom answers it. It works. For the first time in telephone history, a phone call has been placed to Earth from another star system. Next, Tom hangs up and dials 274-7015, the number assigned to Sirius B. The call indeed goes through, and the galactic communications device is a complete success! Tom exclaims his joy and praises them for their fine work.

He informs them that Vega in the Lyran constellation 26 light years away and the Pleiades Cluster 363 light years away will soon be connected. Two other lines will go directly to Sirius B. The other 15 lines will be for local, around-the-farm use for now until Tom may need more in the future.

Robert and his friends and Mr. Mayfield enjoy meeting Tom's crew. They wish each other well, and Tom and his crew teleport back to Sirius B. Mr. Johns declares that his work is finished except for maintenance, and everyone goes home. They agree that this whole project is to remain a secret so as to protect them from government intelligence.

Chapter 7: THE MEETING

13

Nearly a week has passed, and the galactic communications device is in full use. Vega and the Pleiades are already connected, and residents from those star systems are overjoyed to have the ability to communicate directly with Earthlings. Numerous calls are constantly going through, and when Robert would go inside to marvel at the setup, plenty of clicking and clacking sounds from the Strowger switches could be heard.

It is Saturday, March 30, and Robert and his friends have a meeting in the Joslin's woods to discuss their possible plans for the upcoming summer, now that they have the ability to transport themselves by thought. Morris transmits visual images of several extraterrestrial scenes, some that have humans living on them and some that have other lifeforms. Some of them wonder if they are just scenes from some other part of Earth, but Morris insists that they are extraterrestrial scenes. The others are impressed by what Morris can transmit.

They decide to spend time on Sirius B, Vega and the Pleiades, mixing that with some time spent on different places on Earth. What they decide to do is travel with backpacks loaded with as much as ten days of food, and transport back to some place on Earth to restock every week to ten days.

Eight of them can go. Greg and Eric inform them that their schedules won't allow them to join them. Since only the Joslin's, Mr. Johns, and Mr. Mayfield know the truth of the matter, they plan to stage the trip as a road trip out West and plan to actually leave the Joslin's house in Robert's LTD wagon, drive around to the woods entrance, drive back through the woods and into the barn next to it, and hide the car. Steven suggests making things easier by just telling the parents, but Robert talks him out of it, pointing out that most of their parents wouldn't understand and that if too many people found out, it would leak to government intelligence.

They also discuss the issue about telling their possible girlfriends, and they find out among themselves that none of them have any serious girlfriends at this time. Even still, they'll keep it a secret among themselves.

Spring Break comes up in mid April, and James suggests that they go to Cradle Mountain-Lake St. Clair National Park in Tasmania and walk the Overland Track, which runs for 100 kilometers through Tasmania's mountains. They agree that is a great idea and take James up on his suggestion.

After the meeting, they return to the foot of the woods and call Tom from the step office building. Tom teleports down and telepathically gives them the visual images of the telephone stations on Sirius B, Vega, and the Pleiades. Afterwards, Tom wishes them well, inspects the towers and returns to Sirius B. Robert and his friends go home and look forward to Spring Break in Tasmania.

Chapter 8: THE TRIP TO TASMANIA

They eagerly await for Spring Break to arrive. Anyone asking where they are going is told that they are planning a backpacking trip to the mountains of

Georgia. James suggests waiting until they get to Tasmania to purchase food, as the food prices cost around 60% of what they cost in the United States.

Saturday, April 6 comes, and they all meet at Robert's place. They walk to the step office building, and James calls his good friend, Mark Peters, in Devonport, Tasmania and surprises him by telling him that eight of them are coming and will be there in 20 seconds. They transport to his backyard and discover that it's 1 AM Sunday morning, April 7, and James had waked Mark out of bed. Mark, a thin, sort of wiry, black-haired fellow, is surprised beyond belief when he sees a pink glow and hears whirring wind and watches James and his friends materialize in his backyard! They walk inside and explain everything to Mark.

Mark, needless to say, is too excited to go back to bed, and he takes them on a walk around the countryside through the fields and backroads, pointing out the stars and the Bass Strait seen in the distance. Morning finally arrives, and Mark feeds them breakfast, after which he buys their U.S. dollars and sells them Australian ones.

He takes them in his parents' Ford Spectron van to Coles New World and Roelf Vos supermarkets in Devonport, and all of them stock up on food. Robert and Morris decide that this is the place to come once a week this coming summer to stock up on food. The selection is excellent, and the food prices are cheaper. James offers to make the trip each week for all of them, and that would give him a chance to keep up with the news of his home state of Tasmania.

Mark takes them back to his house where they pack their backpacks, and he takes them to the north end of the Overland Track in Cradle Mountain-Lake St. Clair National Park. Mark is unable to join them for the walk, so he leaves them, and James serves as their guide through the whole track for the next week. The weather is decent, and all of them have a great time as they walk through the beautiful, mountainous scenery. Several pet wallabies greet them throughout, and Clinking Currawongs can be seen and heard.

James knows a lot about the trees and points out all of the types as they go along. They notice Eucalyptus trees, King William Pines, Pencil Pines, Celery Top Pines, Southern Sassafras, Leatherwoods, Banksias, Pandanis, and others. They stay in huts along the track each night, and some of the sights they visit are the summit of Cradle Mountain, Lake Windermere, the summit of Mt. Oakleigh, the summit of Mt. Ossa, and Lake St. Clair.

At Lake Windermere, they enjoy meeting Chris and Richard Bell, supposedly from the south of England, only Morris notices that they vanish as they leave to go further up the trail. They realize that they were given a false address, and Morris, James, and Robert have a discussion about the true value of friendship. They speculate as to where Chris and Richard are *really* from, possibly another star system.

The lower half of their walk is more forested and reminds them of the forest in *Snow White and the Seven Dwarfs*. Shortly after reaching Lake St. Clair, they notice some huge Swamp Gums (*Eucalyptus ovata*) up to 3 meters in diameter!

They walk around the west shore of Lake St. Clair and arrive at Cynthia Bay. Plenty of pet wallabies greet them.

James phones his friend, Mark Peters, and he comes to Cynthia Bay in his parents' van, collects them, and takes them to Hobart to visit his uncle. Chris is craving a McDonalds, and Mark informs them that the nearest one is in Melbourne (no McDonalds in Tasmania, and the Tasmanians are proud of it.) In Hobart, they stay overnight at George Peters' place.

The next day, Mark and James take them around Hobart and then Mark drives them up the east coast where they see Maria Island and Freycinet National Park. Then he takes them inland and leaves them at Walls of Jerusalem National Park and returns home.

They ascend through a Gum tree forest and level out in open terrain with plenty of Pencil Pines. Several large mountains occupy the scenery, and they arrive at Dixons Kingdom, the largest pure stand of Pencil Pines in Tasmania. They spend the rest of the day exploring the area, including climbing Mt. Jerusalem. Scenery is excellent.

That evening, they talk with Morris about his crystal ball, and Tom teleports over and pays them a quick visit. He'd been in Launceston re-establishing contact with a non-believing Earth-incarnated Sirian, and he sensed that Morris and his friends were in the vicinity. They camp for the night at Dixons Kingdom forest.

They spend one more day exploring the area and transport themselves from Dixons Kingdom at 11:45 PM and arrive at the Stones River across from Riverdale High School at 7:45 AM Monday, April 15, 1985, just in time. Other friends and peers are told that they had a nice trip down south for Spring Break and nothing more. The truth of where they went remains a secret among them. However, that afternoon, they briefly return to Tasmania with Greg and Eric to show them what they missed.

Chapter 9: ANOTHER VISIT TO RIVERDALE

It is Wednesday, April 24, and they are in Mr. Vance's U.S. history class. They are discussing intelligence levels of different people and cultures, and the discussion shifts to whales and dolphins. Several of them give their opinions. Paul comments that he doesn't *think* any human he knows of has gone down and had a lengthy discussion with a dolphin. A lady whose last name is Childress insists that the sounds they make are indeed communication. Morris comments that humans automatically assume that they are above all other mammals while in fact the cetaceans are *smarter* than the humans. Mr. Tomlin points out that dolphins and whales have no fame and glory because they haven't partaken in wars. Steven says that several dolphins are presently reincarnated as humans. Greg insists that dolphins have no intelligence because he has never seen one with a computer. Morris finishes off the conversation by saying that the dolphins and whales came to Earth 35 million years ago because their old home world was dying, that they used to live as mammals on the land, and that he himself communicates telepathically with them! Paul is certainly surprised! The beep sounds, and they go on to chemistry.

Today, Mr. Mayfield discusses another chapter and gets off the subject and discusses the possibility of people and objects vanishing. Robert and his friends get anxious and hope Mr. Mayfield doesn't spill the beans about the galactic communications device, and they are relieved when the class period is over and he hasn't.

They have lunch, and Morris explains more about the dolphins and their intelligence. He convinces Greg that dolphins don't need computers because they are fully conscious beings. There is a tray on the table, and the principal, Mr. Stockard, asks them to remove it when they leave. After everyone has gone back to class and Robert is the last one left, he takes the tray up, but Mr. Stockard asks him to put it back. He does so and returns to class.

An hour later, the principal calls all of them out of class and has a lengthy discussion with them for nearly half an hour in hopes to get to the bottom of who in the world left that tray on the table! Finally, when Mr. Stockard realizes he cannot get any nearer to his answer, he allows them to return to class. James and Morris comment how ridiculous it is, raising such a fuss over a stupid tray!

Chapter 10: A FEW DAYS IN ENGLAND

A month had passed. School had let out May 24 for summer vacation. Robert, Chris, Morris, and Steven decide to take a trip to England for a few days while waiting for Andrew, James, Paul, and William to finish getting ready for their big travels this summer. They take their bicycles and transport to Cheltenham, Gloucester and meet Malcolm Percival who sells telephones. He sells them a 706 and a 332. Robert briefly returns home to deliver them and then returns to join the others.

They walk their bicycles through the pedestrianized High Street and find a camping store and other stores of interest. Then they ride southeast and cross the Cotswolds Way, cross the A 40 highway, and continue toward Swindon, camping in the yard of some friendly farmers who invite them in to eat supper with them.

The next day, they continue southeast and meet John Ware and his family in Broad Blunsdon. Mr. Ware is a vicar and gives them an impressive tour of the bell tower of his church and then has them over for lunch.

Afterwards, they ride by Swindon and arrive at a farm near Wexcombe and meet Mrs. Forvueweb and her sister Alice. They are nice ladies, and their friend Erica Grinstead comes over in her Ford Transit van and takes them on an evening drive through an old Roman road.

Quite to their surprise, they find out that Mrs. Forvueweb also transports herself to other planets in other star systems by the same method of pink glow and whirring wind. She tells them some stories of where she has been, and she has actually been to Sirius B and Vega. She also tells them of the Planet of the Islands, 3000 light years away.

The next morning, they ride through South Tidworth and then to Stonehenge where they stop and theorize on how the structure got put there and for what purpose. Next, they ride south of Amesbury, enter some woods and transport themselves to northern England just north of Byrness.

They emerge onto the A 69 highway and leave their bicycles with a nearby caravan park and walk north on the Pennine Way to a hut 9 miles up the trail. The terrain is treeless and consists of rolling hills, and the ground is soggy due to the many rainy spells. Wind blows fiercely from the west, and they are relieved to arrive at the small mountain refuge hut.

Chapter 11: THE EARTH MUSEUM

Not long after arriving, Morris gets a strange feeling. Seconds later, two fellows walk in. They are quite astounded. "Chris and Richard Bell!" Robert exclaims. Chris and Richard quickly recall their meeting several weeks ago near Lake Windermere on the Overland Track in Tasmania. Robert and his friends "pin them down" and get to the bottom of where Chris and Richard are really from and find out that they are from the Planet of the Islands and that they actually know Mrs. Forvueweb! Needless to say, Chris and Richard apologize for giving out a false address, explaining that most Earth people freak out at the idea of human beings also living on other star systems.

They explain that they have been unsuccessful in obtaining surplus central office equipment, and that a phone technician and maintenance supervisor went back on their word and wouldn't let them have any equipment. Chris and Richard are ready to throw in the towel on ever obtaining any step office equipment, which they wanted for their Earth museum on their home planet.

Robert and his friends tell them about their recently built galactic communications device and offer to help Chris and Richard obtain what they want. They discuss the particulars, and the next day, they go back to Tennessee with them. They call Tom to help them out, and after some research, discover that the Kingston Park, Georgia step-by-step telephone exchange has just been cut over to digital. Tom helps them set up everything at their museum on the Planet of the Islands. Then he and everyone go to Kingston Park and sneak into the building. The others watch as Tom leaves an anonymous cashier's check on the floor and then literally transports all of the step-by-step equipment out of there and causes it to arrive at the Bell's museum on their home planet, 3000 light years away. The transportation is a success, and they are not caught.

However, the mysterious disappearance of the equipment makes national news the next morning! They are relieved to find that Allied Telecom will not press charges because they were paid for the old equipment via the anonymous cashier's check.

Chapter 12: THE TRIP TO SIRIUS B

It is Monday, June 3, and the eight of them are ready to begin their summer adventures. They all meet at Robert Joslin's place, load up his Ford LTD wagon, leave as the other parents see them off, drive around to the woods entrance, go through the woods, check to be sure no one is watching, emerge from the woods, enter the barn, and hide the car in the barn, surrounding it with hay bales. Next, they *really* leave on their trip and transport to Sirius B, a planet with around 20 million human beings living on it.

They arrive to a hot sunny day and discover that the terrain is desert-like and that the soil is mostly red in color. Cypress-Pines, Tamarisk shrubs and Cactus plants dot the hilly terrain. They see the telephone station a short distance away, walk over to it, and meet Manta, the operator. She sends for Tom who teleports over and takes them to his house which is underground.

They eat supper with him, and his friend Caymar comes over and tells them about the mountains of the far north. He offers to accompany them up there, and the next day they transport there, several thousand kilometers away. Tom cannot come because he has some galactic trading to take care of.

Caymar and the others arrive at the plains at the foot of a huge mountain which towers 5000 meters over them. Some of them feel reluctant to climb all the way, but the more energetic ones talk the rest of them into the adventure and challenge. They start the long climb which takes them 2½ days. The terrain is somewhat wet with plenty of water seeping out of the ground in many places. They camp in a shady cove for the night.

The next day, they continue higher, passing through a narrow crevice to access the higher slopes which they ascend to reach a stone hut that Caymar and his friends built several years ago. Just before reaching the hut, they hear the most awful roar from higher up the mountain. It's a rock storm! They run for it and manage to reach the hut just in time and take shelter on the downhill side of it. Some of boulders barely miss some of them! From their now safe position, they watch the rocks go whizzing further downhill and crashing way below, where they had just been. It was a narrow escape. After getting over their shock, they go inside and camp for the night.

The next morning, Caymar takes them to the high summit which is an old volcanic crater. They play in the snow-filled crater for a while and then descend into a river gorge on the mountain's other side. They camp for the night. From there, they climb into the next range and reach a large lake, the largest one on Sirius B. They rest a day and do some exploring around the area and do some fishing, as well.

They continue for several more days, seeing more mountainous scenery and finally descend a different gorge back into the plains at the foot of the mountains. They transport back to Tom's residence and tell him all about it. Tom shrugs and shakes his head when they tell him about the rock storm, and he tells them he does not approve of Caymar's choice of location for the hut.

There is a city called Ahntraytitral around 100 kilometers away. It's population is around 50,000, and Tom has set up homestays for the teenagers. They transport there, and Tom delivers them to several families to stay with for several days. They enjoy their stays and learn more about Sirian culture. There are no TV's, no radios, no newspapers, and therefore no bad news. The city has no banks, no police stations, no law offices, no government buildings, no commercial establishments, no fuel stations, and so on. The Sirians just don't need all of that stuff, as they are truly honest and trustworthy people.

Several days later, Tom returns to collect them and takes them to another part of Sirius B and gives them a tour of the storage facilities and warehouses. He informs Robert that they are thinking of adding more lines to the galactic communications device. After the tour, they thank Tom and transport to Tasmania to purchase more food. They briefly visit Mark while there.

Chapter 13: THE TRIP TO VEGA

Vega, according to Tom, also has humans living on it, and it is very similar to Sirius B. It is another hot, dry planet with the same types of plants as what grow on Sirius B, only this planet is hotter! They arrive and find the telephone station nearby and meet Ingra, and she tells them about Vega and informs them that Eucalyptus trees also grow here. She transports herself with them to the edge of the Eucalyptus forest and leaves them there.

The eight of them take off walking for several days through constant Eucalyptus forest, glad to be out of the heat of the star Vega. They camp in the forest for the night at the top of a hill, and Morris and the others get to talking about the origins of Earth humans and that they likely were transported here in ape form, evolved for a while, and then returned to Earth between 1 and 2 million years ago.

That night, Morris has an interesting dream, and the next morning, he tells the others all about it. He was talking to a Eucalyptus tree, and it told him that they arrived on Earth 35 million years ago and actually came with the dolphins from their old home world Delikadove whose star was Danetar and was 45,000 light years distant. It also told Morris that the land dolphins were called dolphs and that they had a symbiotic relationship with a silicon-based lifeform called Shakeilar. Everyone is astounded at Morris' dream, and James verifies that he knows that Eucalyptus trees suddenly came on the scene in Earth's fossil record 35 million years ago. So, they determine that Morris could, in actual fact, be correct.

They continue walking through the forest and find a much welcomed water hole and fill their canteens. Then they notice a glass igloo and discover that it is a Shakeilar shelter. Inside lives a man named Lyro, a fairly indifferent and eccentric man who explains that Vega is the only planet where both the Shakeilar and the humans live in a symbiotic relationship. After talking to them a few minutes, he just goes back inside his shelter, and that's it. Robert and his friends feel turned away and continue through the forest. Morris explains that they are not as welcome on this planet as they were on Sirius B.

Finally, the next day, they emerge into a hot, treeless terrain and make their way toward a distant speck of light on the horizon. They find a canyon and camp at its bottom by the river, enjoying the water and the swimming.

The next day, they climb out of the canyon and finally reach the speck of light which is actually a large glass dome, a Shakeilar city, Morris theorizes. As soon as James reaches out to touch it, it suddenly vanishes! James and the others are really angry and feel put off. They ask Morris to explain why this happened, and he plays difficult and refuses. The others plead with Morris, and he gets angry at them. They push and shove and finally pin Morris down and get him to talk, and he reveals to them why it disappeared.

Morris then apologizes to the others and explains the troubles he had during his childhood. With that said, they decide to leave Vega and transport to the top of the knob in the Joslin's woods.

Chapter 14: THE TRIP TO THE PLEIADES

They meet in the woods and wait for sunrise. James transports to Devonport and buys food for everyone while the others wait and decide to visit the Pleiades. Once James returns, they transport to Aleyone, the only planet in the Pleiades cluster with life on it. They arrive near the telephone station in the middle of a lush and primitive looking Fern-Palm tree forest. They meet Suzanne, a young princess, as she calls herself.

She explains to them about their way of life on Aleyone and how the Pleiadeans had an influence on Earth 6000 years ago. As she talks to them, she soon developes special interest in James, tells him he's cute, and flirts with him, causing him to blush. The others joke with him that the love bug is biting him. James angrily bursts out at them, and Morris calms him down. Suzanne has a big laugh about it all, seeing how Earthlings lose their temper over so little.

Suzanne relates some of the history of Aleyone to them, saying that it is an older star system that was caught up in a newer system that formed 60 million years ago. She tells them that it was quite an engineering feat they performed to save their planet and star system 60 million years ago, but they made it through unharmed.

Next, she walks them to her parents' house, which is nestled in the edge of the Fern-Palm forest by the river, and they meet her family. Her parents are Michael and Carya, and her brother is Harvey. They have supper with them and spend the night. That evening, Michael, who is a healer, gives them rocks and crystals, including a green Fluorite crystal ball which he gives to Morris.

The next day, they tour the city of Towdenmore across the river. It is the only city on Aleyone. They don't want any more cities, as they want all of their industry and manufacturing in one location to save on transporting costs. Only 90,000 people live on the planet of Aleyone. They find the city very interesting. Michael takes them into one office building, and aren't they surprised to see Virginia, the lady from the stone hut on Lopeia! She is equally as surprised and explains that she transports here every so often to do work with Earthlings on the dream level.

Next, Michael gives them a tour of the manufacturing facilities where they see all kinds of products being manifested, grown, casted, and assembled. They even watch spacecrafts being made. Much of what is made is traded with civilizations throughout the whole galaxy. After the tour, he escorts them back to the river side and they cross back over to his house.

Not long after returning, the phone rings, and Michael goes inside the house to answer it. He comes back outside and informs them that it was Tom, that he has a project for them, and is going to teleport here.

Seconds later, he arrives in their backyard. He has another mission for them, this one to find a lost ancient crystal stolen from Atlantis over 15,000 years ago. The others listen with interest as Tom explains that once that exotic crystal was stolen from Atlantis, the people went downhill from the flourishing and advanced race that they were. They lost their sense of preservation and developed greed, did genetic experiments, and more. Finally, their continent was destroyed when they sank.

Tom goes on to explain that whoever stole the crystal likely dropped it off on another star system for fear of being caught, and he feels almost certain that it is somewhere on Aleyone. He explains that the crystal was basically greenish-blue, was grown in the shape of an egg, and had an orange pyramidal-shaped crystal within it. It was grown by a pre-Atlantean civilization that used to live in what is now Antarctica.

All eight of them get interested and want to begin the treasure hunt right away. Tom leaves them with the mission and teleports back to Sirius B. They go inside with Michael, and they go over several maps in hopes of determining the most likely area in which the crystal could be hidden. They decide that the most likely place may be an island in the oceans in the southern hemisphere of Aleyone.

After spending another night at Michael and Carya's house, they transport there. Suzanne and Harvey accompany them, and they arrive at the edge of a beach which is lined by a very thick, prehistoric looking forest of Lepidodendrons, Calamites, Palms, and Cycads. It appears impenetrable, but they manage to make their way through it and have a difficult time with it. Some of them grumble and complain about it. Finally, after several hours, the going gets easier, and the forest is more open at higher altitude.

They camp in a grassy meadow for the night, and continue on the next day. Four days pass, and they have now arrived at the high mountains and enter an alpine meadow lined with Archeaopteris trees, which look somewhat like Baldcypress trees. They set up camp in the grove on the upper end of the meadow.

While resting, Robert hears a telepathic message and listens as he realizes that the trees are talking! Harvey and Suzanne also listen. The Archaeopteris trees know that the exotic crystal is nearby and up in the mountains. Robert is astounded that he could hear a telepathic message, his first time ever. That night he comes up with a phrase: *land line connect.*

The next morning, he tells the others about the strange phrase, and Paul solves the riddle and realizes that it means ledge because the flat surface and the wall *connect* at the *land line*. With that new information at hand, the search is narrowed, and all of them set out into the mountains in pairs and search every cliff and ledge for the exotic crystal. Robert and Andrew actually find the crystal buried next to several Archaeopteris trees and return to camp. When the others arrive, they certainly are surprised!

They take several Archaeopteris seedlings at the request of their parent trees and return to Michael and Carya's house. Robert phones Tom and tells him the great news. Michael looks at the crystal and receives a telepathic message: *Land line connect, Timpanogos.* The others think it over, and William recalls that name, Timpanogos and informs them that it is a mountain in Utah. They decide to go there and place the crystal on one of its ledges.

All of them thank Michael and Carya and say they will soon return to see more.

EPILOGUE

They arrive in an alpine meadow on the slopes of Mt. Timpanogos near Orem and Provo, Utah. What they do is climb further up the mountain, find a nice ledge high up on a cliff, and transport up to it. There, they place the crystal on the soil and plant several Archaeopteris seedlings. Their mission is accomplished, and now they can only hope that the exotic crystal will do its work and cause the people of Earth to wake up and take care of the environment and become better friends with each other. They predict that the United States and the Soviet Union will one day be friends.

With that, they transport to the bottom of the cliff and climb to the summit of Mt. Timpanogos, enjoy the views, and return to a stone hut to camp for the night in one of the higher meadows. A rain storm comes, and they see a double complete rainbow which symbolizes a better future for planet Earth. Morris receives a telepathic message about Antarctica, something about.....

Summary and Synopsis of:
MISSION BEYOND THE ICE CAVE: Atlantis-Mexico-Zotola
written by: Robert S. Sanders, Jr., 1996-1998

How can meeting some fellows from the Orion star system and visiting an ice cave in Antarctica cause some teenagers to unravel the mysterious disappearance of Atlantis?

Introduction and Character Sketch

This novel, MISSION BEYOND THE ICE CAVE: Atlantis-Mexico-Zotola, takes place in the summer of 1985 and is the continuation of MISSION OF THE GALACTIC SALESMAN. The same teenagers have been enjoying their summer travels, and as this sequel opens, they are called to visit Antarctica, the frozen former homeland of what used to be Atlantis. They transport there and by chance meet up with two fellows, Rinto and Fraxino Zapatero, who suddenly arrive in their vehicle-craft from the star Al Nitak in the Orion Belt. They have come to do some research of their Atlantean heritage, and they explore an ice cave together. Venture with them as they discover what the cave walls contain.

Six of the eight characters go home with them to the land of Zotola, home to many of the descendants of Atlantis. They live in a city called Zantaayer, a beautiful, clean city nestled within the Ciruclar Mountains and situated on the northern coast of Zotola. Their society is on the same level of technological advancement as their cousins on Earth. However, the air is crisp and clear because there are no fossil fuels used, since they never had a coal age.

Two more characters go home early in the story, leaving Andrew, Chris, Robert, and Steven to enjoy the fun and adventures with their new friends.

With Rinto and Fraxino Zapatero, they become very good friends. They are wizards to say the least, and they have an uncanny ability to interpret crystals, grow them, and harness their knowledge and intelligence to operate their vehicle-craft, their computer system, and ultimately to fulfill a mission in Mexico. Rinto is more into mechanics and personally modified a Zotolan Velosa cruiser craft so they could use it to teleport to other worlds. Fraxino, with his interest and enthusiasm for rocks and minerals, has his input with creating the on-board main controls crystal.

Chispo Colancha is a lively character, always full of spark and enthusiasm. He is Rinto and Fraxino's nearby neighbor and good friend, and he quickly joins the others in all of their activities. His ability to interpret and perceive messages stored within crystals and holographic materials is well above the norm, nearly as fine tuned as Rinto and Fraxino's abilities. He and Robert Joslin quickly become close friends and are astounded at the synchronicities by which they meet. Chispo also helps Robert discover the mysterious origin of the Liriodendrons, the Tulip Poplars.

25

With Chispo's suggestion, they travel to an ancient galactic dump site in a desert valley south of Zantaayer, where they uncover a large crate of holographic metal plates evidently brought in by the Atlanteans when they came to their new world 12,500 years ago. Find out what they contain when Rinto, Fraxino, and Chispo later examine them on their crystal base computer system.

Tom, the galactic salesman, comes forth with another mission. He wants to establish telephone communication with their world, but he discovers an obstacle. Communication with the Orion Belt is blocked. He offers them a hefty reward. Can they, with the help of Rinto, Fraxino, and Chispo, succeed in pinpointing and eliminating the problem to clear the mysterious block?

Venture with them as they travel to the mountains of southern Zotola and meet an ancient endemic race of green humans. Find out what their culture has to offer and how they are linked both to Atlantis and to Mexico.

Follow them as they travel to northern Mexico where they analyze some ancient paintings, make new friends, discover more coincidences, and have numerous adventures which include exploring and searching the slopes of Mexico's mountains.

Chapter 1: MESSAGE FROM ANTARCTICA

The story opens in late June, 1985 on the slopes of Mt. Timpanogos in Utah. Morris has just heard a strange telepathic message about Antarctica, something about a civilization that used to live there and that there were a few of them that never left. Morris informs them that once the exotic crystal was stolen, everything went downhill. The Earth slid. The seas rose. Everything flooded and then froze. All was lost. The message Morris was hearing fades.

They ponder on what Morris has just heard, and they determine that the message came from the exotic crystal they had just left on the cliff ledge on Mt. Timpanogos. They transport themselves up to the ledge to see if they can get more of the message, and Morris receives a visual image of a white landscape which they determine to be Antarctica.

Then Morris gets a strange additional message saying, "60375 . . . Go meet him."

They wonder what that has to do with anything, and Robert shows a look of surprise because those five digits match a number Robert had dialled in a dream when he went to call Morris, dialling 896-0375 instead of his correct number of 896-0278 in the dream. All they can determine is that Robert was meant to have that dream. Maybe the exotic crystal had put that number in Robert's mind when he dreamed it.

Morris goes ahead and telepathically transmits the cold, white Antarctic scene to everyone else so that they can transport themselves there. Then they transport themselves back to the stone hut where they camp for the night and prepare supper.

They start discussing the concepts of Earth crustal displacement, and Morris explains that the whole shell of the Earth very well could have slid 2,000 miles some 12,500 years ago, due to an imbalance of the glacial ice weight at the poles. Steven suddenly figures it out and explains to the others that the centrifugal force of the spinning earth would literally cause the ice to slide toward the equator, pulling the whole of the Earth's crust along with it. As a result, Antarctica was sent 2,000 miles further south to its present location around the South Pole.

They speculate that the results must have been disastrous with tidal waves, earthquakes, and the rest of it. Mammoths were almost instantly frozen when they were suddenly sent to the arctic. The whole process may have only taken a few days. Some of them, especially Andrew, doubt the whole process.

They realize that Antarctica may be what used to be Atlantis since Atlantis was always considered to be in the middle of the ocean and since Atlantis did somewhat sink since the oceans rose. It makes sense to them the more they think about it.

Robert and William transport themselves back to Tennessee long enough to gather some warm clothes for everyone, and they return later that night to camp with the others in the stone hut.

The next morning, they transport themselves away to Antarctica.

Chapter 2: THE ICE CAVE IN ANTARCTICA

They arrive to a cold scene and find themselves standing on a large sheet of ice and windswept snow. It is very cold, and the wind is howling. They briefly see some Emperor penguins sliding by on their bodies and using their flippers to move themselves along.

To get out of the cold wind, they transport themselves over to some mountains in the distance and are relieved to find the wind hardly blowing at all. Andrew spots a cave up the mountain slope and suggests that they climb the slope to investigate it. They begin climbing.

Suddenly, only a few minutes after they begin their climb, they hear a strange humming noise and then notice some sort of a craft sitting on the icy plains below them. It is mostly green in color with a tinge of yellow, and it has four wheels. It doesn't look too different from a futuristic car or van.

They cautiously ponder calling out to it. Then they see two human fellows emerge from the craft, and when the two of them notice the others, Robert calls out to them. The anxiety is over when they return a friendly reply in English. They catch up to the others and introduce themselves as Rinto and Fraxino Zapatero from Zotola on the planet Artenia around the star Al Nitak, the bottom star of the three stars of the Orion Belt. They live on the outskirts of a city called Zantaayer, which is situated by a coast, but also nestled at the base of the Ciruclar Mountains, which surround the city on three sides.

They explain that they are descendants of the people of Atlantis, who fled Antarctica to settle a new world 12,500 years ago when Atlantis suffered a devastating natural disaster. Rinto and Fraxino explain that they have come to research their ancestral roots for a history project. They also explain that they know English because they have made previous visits to Earth over the past year, ever since they completed their cruiser craft project. They surprise them by saying that they had actually spent some time in Tennessee and that their next door neighbor had spent even more time in Tennessee.

As they climb the slope, Robert and his friends explain to Rinto and Fraxino about their involvement with a galactic salesman named Tom and that they had helped him by building a galactic communications device, after which they had been enjoying their summer travels.

They reach the cave and enter it together. The warmth is a welcome relief from the cold. They proceed down a corridor and descend some stairs and reach a wall of ice. On the solid ice-free wall opposite it, they discover rows and rows of hieroglyphic inscriptions with numerous rocks and crystals interspersed throughout the text.

They talk with Morris about what the inscriptions say, and he says that they are a very impressive display of what is likely an accurate historical record of Atlantis.

Suddenly, Morris gets a very strong feeling that he's not supposed to know something he's about to find out, and he informs them he has to abandon the group and leave. He claims that Rinto is linked to something he's not supposed to know about until he has done considerable dolphin research. He informs them his next calling is to research the dolphins.

The others question him with surprise, and Morris insists that he must leave. He seems to have a touch of anger. He talks briefly with Rinto and Fraxino. He leaves with Robert the green Fluorite crystal ball that Michael on Aleyone had given him, saying for him to give it to someone he will soon meet and that he will know who he is when the time is right. He says farewell to everyone and transports himself away.

Rinto and Fraxino offer to take them home to their world.

James decides this is as good a time as any, and he transports himself away to the Pleiades. He misses Suzanne.

Once those two are gone, Rinto begins to read and interpret the hieroglyphic inscriptions, and he takes out a piece of orange Calcite and telepathically scans in the data stored in the rocks and crystals interspersed throughout the text.

They jokingly tell everyone that what they are doing is something Morris is not yet supposed to know about.

Rinto does indeed verify that Atlantis slid to the South Pole during the devastating Earth crustal displacement. Andrew begins believing that maybe continents can move after all.

As they leave the ice cave, Rinto informs them that Al Nitak is 1,132 light years away from Earth. They descend the mountain slope and reach the vehicle-craft on the icy plains.

Rinto and Fraxino describe their vehicle-craft to them, saying that it is made out of a mixture of various metals including Vanadium, mixed with a silicon base. The body is grown over a period of several months. Inside, the controls are very similar to an automobile's controls, with a steering wheel and a 5-speed gear shift. In addition to that, there is a main controls crystal cube made out of Ulexite along with a crystal array of various crystals. The craft is made by a Zotolan company called Velosa, and the vehicle-craft is called a Velosa cruiser craft. The internal combustion engine runs on hydrogen fuel, and it has zero emissions.

They climb aboard, and Rinto starts the engine. He proceeds along, and he soon switches off the engine and pulls back a lever, now using the power and intelligence of the crystal array. They leave the ground. Fraxino explains that the crystal array was grown with slight impurities added which were needed to give the crystals their capacity for intelligence so they could counter gravity and fly. With the right combination of added impurities, the etheric minds of the crystals become very clear as they are tuned to the right vibrational frequencies.

They have picked up speed, and now that they are flying well above the ground, they feel a forcefield accompanied by a faint green glow overcome them, and they briefly dematerialize. Before they totally realize it, they find themselves looking out of the windows at a blue-green world which isn't Earth, even though it looks similar at a glance.

Chapter 3: THE TRIP TO ZANTAAYER

Rinto explains that the crystal array is so smart that it can teleport them anywhere they want to go. They think of the place, and the crystals read their thoughts, activate, and teleport them there.

Rinto and Fraxino comment how lucky they are to have found those cave wall inscriptions. They also describe the features and characteristics of Artenia, saying that their year is 423 of their days long with 25½ Earth hours per day. They have almost the same gravity at 98%. Zantaayer is situated at a latitude of 40° north.

As they are approaching the coast of Zotola, Fraxino takes a holographic disk out of a box and inserts it into a player. Music similar to pop music is soon heard to play. The young pop artists are called *The Hydragyros*, and they are from Zantaayer. Their music is so moving and invigorating to Robert and his friends that they are gripped with an uncanny sense of familiarity.

The album plays through the songs as Rinto lowers the altitude of the craft and brings them in for a landing on a forested gravel road at the top of the Ciruclar Mountains west of Zantaayer. Trees whiz by as he touches down on the winding road. Over the next half hour, he drives them down the winding gravel road descending the mountain. Zantaayer can be seen through the trees, and the air is so crisp and clear.

Once at the bottom of the mountain, the pavement begins, and Rinto drives them the few kilometers to their house where the Zapateros live. Their parents are home because Rinto and Fraxino's father's antique classic turquoise *Tolejo* sedan is parked in the driveway. Once Rinto parks, they step out of the vehicle-craft into the crisp and clear air. Rinto and Fraxino take them inside and introduce them to their parents. They don't speak English.

The sound of gravel can be heard next door, and Rinto realizes that Chispo, his neighbor has arrived. He and Fraxino take everyone over there, and they meet Chispo. He is just stepping out of a smooth, futuristic-looking golden yellow car called a *Velva Dibe*.

Rinto introduces them, saying they're from Tennessee, and Chispo perks up with interest. He is a lively person with spark and enthusiasm, and Robert, more than the others, finds him familiar. He introduces himself as Chispo Colancha-Pachanga and informs them that Rinto's full name is Rinto Zapatero-Rodiga. Chispo also informs them that he is the one who went to Tennessee last year and went to school there. He says he had a great time in Tennessee.

He joins them, and they walk back over to the Zapateros where Rinto and Fraxino show everyone the workings of their Velosa cruiser craft, including the Richmond in-line 6-cylinder motor and the Ulexite cube and crystal array.

Chispo tells them they would have laughed if they could have seen all the junk that Rinto and Fraxino dragged home from the mountains when they worked on the cruiser craft project, growing the crystal array and giving the crystals their intelligence to fly the craft, and to teleport to other worlds! Chispo says he was really impressed when it actually worked.

They decide to drive up into the mountains and show them the cave where they have their crystal growing room and where they grew their crystal array for the project. Mrs. Zapatero asks Rinto and Fraxino to return home in time so Rinto can mow the lawn before dark. She also complains about all the junk they have dragged home.

On the way, they stop by an Exxoll station to fuel up. Everyone is surprised to see the name of the fuel company appear in Earth's alphabet, and they comment how similar it is to *Exxon*. The price of hydrogen is presently 11.6 duocibols per liter. There are 144 duocibols per Zotolan zúbola, which is worth the equivalent of just over US $6.

Fraxino drives them back up the mountain, and at the ridge top, they park and hike down a gully to access a cave entrance. They enter the cave, and over ten minutes, Rinto and Fraxino take them back to a nearly inaccessible room where they grow their crystals. They also explain about their unique crystallized protection security system which telepathically prevents would-be intruders from going to that area of the cave.

They show them the room and their setup, and then they return to the entrance and hike back up the gully to the vehicle-craft.

On the way, they get to talking about a site around 100 kilometers south of Zantaayer where they look for crystals. Chispo insists that the site is an ancient galactic dump site, even though Rinto doesn't believe it has all that much significance.

Rinto drives them back to the Zapateros, and they eat supper with them. Quite to their surprise, they discover that Mr. Zapatero can suddenly speak English! He has suddenly acquired it off the minds of Rinto and Fraxino's friends from Tennessee.

While eating supper, Mr. Zapatero (Glecko) explains the story behind Exxoll, saying that though only a few of Earth's top officials know this, 15 years ago Earth's *Exxon* company expanded to a galactic level and bought a monopoly on their hydrogen fuel companies and set up their business on Artenia under the name of Exxoll. They did it to monitor and research the selling of hydrogen fuel.

After supper, Chispo talks to Robert and asks him to come over to his house, that he has something to show him. Robert, who had found Chispo familiar, goes with him, and once at his house, he shows Robert an interesting crystal with a ghostly image of a Pine cone within, when viewed at certain angles in the light. It also has 7 equatorial rings around it and numerous stars dotting its surface. Chispo also astounds Robert with his intuition about how much he intuitively knows about him and his group.

As Robert looks at the crystal, he realizes that the green Fluorite crystal Morris had given him was intended for Chispo. As it turns out, they exchange crystals and realize that they were meant to meet. Chispo reads the crystal pretty well and impresses Robert with his accuracy.

31

As they talk, Chispo speculates that the Pine cone crystal was grown over 100,000 years ago in what is now Antarctica. That technologically advanced civilization used to grow crystals regularly.

The phone rings, and Chispo goes to answer it. Robert hadn't realized that Artenia had phone service. As he and Chispo discuss the phone system, Chispo explains that all of it is on step-by-step, which comes as a surprise to Robert. Artenia's phone company is called Astrelcom.

Robert tells Chispo the weird message that Morris heard about "60375, go meet him." Chispo is very surprised and informs Robert that 60375 is his phone number!

Chispo realizes they were definitely meant to meet, and they realize how interesting destiny is. They determine that the crystals set up the coincidence so they would meet each other and exchange crystals.

They talk about the phone system, about the ancient galactic dump site, and Chispo also shows Robert his Velva Dibe with its Richmond V-8 engine and the 4-speed manual transmission. Chispo explains that Zantaayer makes numerous products used throughout Artenia, and also cars such as Glecko's classic Tolejo sedan, and other cars such as the Skiivona.

They return to the Zapateros, and they inform them of the coincidences and synchronicities they discovered. They visit for a while. Chispo tells everyone about the Day of Cresma on their world. Cresma was a heroic man in Artenian history. It was he who organized the arrival of more than 65,000 Atlantean settlers to planet Artenia, upon which the city of Zantaayer was founded. In honor of Cresma and his achievements, the Day of Cresma is observed the first day of each year. In Artenian years, they are in the year 10130, which in Earth years, would be 12,500.

Rinto shows them his crystal base computer system. They read in from the piece of orange Calcite the information they gathered in the ice cave. They talk about it, and they eventually go to sleep.

The next day, they decide to go to the ancient galactic dump site. Paul had a disturbing dream, and he informs them he has to go home. William accompanies him, and the two of them transport themselves away.

The seven of them: Andrew, Chris, Robert, Steven, Rinto, Fraxino, and Chispo, take off in the vehicle-craft, driving through Zantaayer's central district, then crossing over the Ciruclar Mountains, and reaching the ancient galactic dump site an hour later.

Chapter 4: THE ANCIENT GALACTIC DUMP SITE

The scenery around them is a field of boulders with a range of mountains called the Placatera Mountains to the southwest. They step out of the vehicle-craft, and they begin searching for rocks and crystals of different colors.

Andrew makes a suggestion that they look not just on the surface of the ground but that they also dig. There might be a lot more interesting things buried beneath the surface. As Chispo and Robert talk about the Pine cone crystal, Rinto and Fraxino take Andrew's suggestion and return to the vehicle-craft to fetch their digging tools.

While the others do their searching, Chispo takes Robert over the the spot where he had found the Pine cone crystal. He and Robert search for more crystals, and Robert turns up another egg-shaped crystal. As Robert wipes the dirt off of it, they notice that it has an image of a Tulip Poplar cone within it. As Chispo recognizes it, he calls it the Flowering Sun Tree.

As they are talking about it, they suddenly hear a shout in the distance from where the others are. Chispo responds, and one of them shouts back that they have just discovered a bunch of holographic plates. Chispo and Robert rush over to the others, quickly hopping from boulder to boulder as they go. They reach them in five minutes.

Both of them are surprised as they see the others inspecting a bunch of black metal plates, likely made out of bronze. Each plate contains a bluish-purple smooth surface on one side. Most of the plates are still sitting inside the large metal box they have just unearthed.

Robert shows the others what he just found, and Andrew is the first one to look at it. He recognizes the image of the Tulip Poplar cone inside.

Chispo starts checking out the holographic plates, laughs in amazement, and as he views one of them, he suspects that the plates may contain some ancient data, possibly for image processing or for data storage. Some of them might have been used to give instructions to computers like modern disk drives do on computers back on Earth. The plates may very well have been used in conjunction with an ancient computer system. As they continue inspecting the plates, they get the strong feeling that the plates came from Earth, possibly from the days of Atlantis, and that they possibly tell a history of Earth's earlier civilizations.

Chispo reads the plates better than anyone else, and he comments that he just probes himself into the plates, extending his mind into them, and the thoughts just come to him.

They carry the plates and the box to the vehicle-craft, and on the way, Robert notices an orange piece of crystal lying on the ground. It's a piece of orange Calcite around 15 centimeters in size. He picks it up, and he shows it to Steven. When Robert turns over the crystal, he is very surprised to see rows of what appear to be holographic filmstrips firmly attached to a smooth flat side of the piece of Calcite. Steven inspects it with a questioning reaction.

Chispo expresses interest, and as he looks at it, he laughs in amazement. He declares that it's an ancient holographic filmstrip, and he informs them that they come from Lyra, that is, Vega. Legend has it that the ancestors of the Atlanteans colonized Earth from Vega long before Atlantis was founded, and they believe the holographic filmstrips to be around 150,000 to 200,000 years old. Each stone was thought to tell a sacred story.

As Chispo concentrates, he proceeds to tell everyone the story on the piece of holographic filmstrip. Quite to Chispo's surprise and also everyone else's, the filmstrip relates a sacred story about the Tulip Poplars.

The Flowering Sun Tree or as they call it on Earth, the Tulip Poplar, is a sacred tree endemic to Vega, and the early humans that first colonized Earth 1 to 2 million years ago brought that tree species with them as a reminder of their home world. The tree is very fast growing, grows to great size, is virtually disease free, has wood which is easily workable, and is a superior tree in many respects.

The leaves have a different and unique method of growing, and each flower has a sunshine in its cup. From the inner part of the flower to the outer part, the colors change from yellow to orange to green. The sun in its yellow center gives forth through the orange flames to the green of life . . . the forest. To early humans, this was very sacred.

As Chispo relates the rest of the story, they discover that the early humans arrived with the tree species to what is now China and that the tree species arrived to eastern North America by a much more exotic method, that they were accidentally teleported there from China when some guru among them accidentally caused a whole forest of them to disappear in China.

Andrew actually brings up the fact that in Vicksburg, Mississippi the soil is different, and the only matching soil is in . . . China!

Chris manages to point out that the scientific name for the Tulip Poplar is

Liriodendron. The word Lirio comes from the Greek word Leirion which is very similar to the word Lyran which is the name of the constellation Vega is in. Sometimes the older languages have more sense to them than is realized.

Further, there are only two species of *Liriodendron* in the world, and the species literally sits by itself in its classification. Robert feels somewhat astounded and beside himself at what he has just found out about the Tulip Poplars.

They finish carrying the holographic plates to the vehicle-craft, and Rinto drives them back to their home in Zantaayer.

Glecko and Sosta greet them as they are carrying the heavy bronze metal box full of plates into the house. Meanwhile, Robert shows Glecko the egg-shaped clear quartz crystal with the image of the Tulip Poplar cone within, and then he shows him the piece of orange Calcite. Glecko remarks with considerable interest that it's a sacred story stone from Lyra.

Once Rinto and Fraxino open the lid of the bronze metal box, Glecko remarks with even more interest that they *really* made a find this time. He and Chispo agree that it would be a good idea to keep it away from Zotola's news media.

As Rinto places the first plate on the tray of the crystal base computer, they discover that the set of plates were put together by an Atlantean historical society dedicated to preserving its heritage and technology. It was done 10,130 Artenian years ago, shortly after the devastating Earth crustal displacement. Andrew finally admits that the crustal displacement indeed took place.

There are 144 plates altogether, and plates 101 - 144 are entirely dedicated to programming instructions for their state of the art computers of that time. The rest of the plates, 1 - 100, document Atlantean history, speculation, and various types of philosophy and other odd phenomena of the human species.

The first plate they look at is plate number 36: *Origin of the Hieroglyphics.* It reveals that early humans who first colonized Earth from Vega communicated mostly by mental telepathic imagery, that they transmitted visual images back and forth to each other. Around 150,000 years ago, a new line of humans was being born who could not communicate so well by telepathy. The Lyrans set up their Earthly cousins with a spoken language, and they derived around 2,000 of the most common visual images, and set them up through a computer system which the people used to transmit the images back and forth to each other as a form of communication.

Over time, the images became computer icons. The people would make sentences out of them. Over the generations, the icons were simplified and became hieroglyphics. Through time, they evolved to the written text languages of the modern world.

It further goes on to reveal that by 32,500 years ago, the Neanderthal man became replaced by the new line of non-telepathic humans, with a small percentage of the new line of humans retaining their telepathic abilities.

Rinto, Fraxino, Chispo, and the others discuss and realize that while hieroglyphics were very efficient in some ways, there must have been a destined plan for written text languages to come about. While a picture can tell a thousand words, it's not always as precise nor specific as written text languages can describe it.

Paul and William return briefly and inform them that they have to return to Earth and quit travelling with the group. Paul's father has a crisis at the plant, and William has to begin working for his father with the phone company to save money for college which is a little more than a year away. The others say goodbye to them and see them off, and they take home all of the winter clothing and gear that they had used in Antarctica. Chispo assures Robert and his friends that they will continue to accompany them for the rest of the summer.

They return to the crystal base computer and view another holographic plate, plate number 44: *End of Atlantis, Leaving, Reminiscent of the Human Beginnings*. As the translated text appears on the screen, Rinto narrates that many residents of Atlantis were experiencing premonitions and that they started making preparations to flee to another world. They knew that the third planet out from the star Al Nitak was one of the original cradles of human civilizations. Chispo is surprised to read on the screen that the human species goes back 72 million years!

65,000 Atlantean residents fled Earth and returned to Al Nitak via spacecrafts. The original human stock naturally evolved on the third planet out from Al Nitak, and when they achieved technologically advanced status, they began to travel to other star systems. They didn't settle Earth until just a few million years ago.

When the Atlanteas fled to Al Nitak, they left around 400 residents on Earth to spread their culture around that planet. Many were top scientists, and they engineered and built many artifacts around the world, including the great pyramids.

Quite to everyone's surprise, the plate reveals that Al Nitak is only 76.3 light years away, not the believed 1,132 light years. Robert and his friends watch as Chispo, Rinto, and Fraxino discuss the obvious discrepancy. They determine that it must be a recent government cover-up scheme to keep people from thinking there was life in the Orion Belt. Rinto checks the data he collected in the ice cave in Antarctica, and sure enough, it gives the star system distance as 76.37 light years from Earth's Sol system.

As a result of this revelation about the true distance between Al Nitak and the Sol system, Rinto and Fraxino decide to go to Zantaayer's central library to investigate the discrepancy. Everyone leaves in the vehicle-craft, and while Rinto and Fraxino do their research in the library, Chispo takes them on a tour of the city's central district. They visit some markets, and Robert buys a holodisk of *The Hydragyros*. Next, Chispo takes them to the beach on the north side of the city, and then he takes them to the University of Zotola.

There on the campus, the word *Hichicera* is telepathically revealed to Robert, and he also sees within his mind an image of a crystal with a scene of mountains within. Chispo picks up some telepathic data about a race of green men living in some remote mountains in southern Zotola.

They return to the library and Rinto and Fraxino have indeed found that in some of the more ancient texts, the listed distance between Al Nitak and the Sol system is between 75 and 80 light years.

They return to the house, and they look at more holographic plates including plate number 45: *Speculation on Future Human Philosophy Based on Atlantean Views*. Rinto narrates the text which says that the human species is not originally from planet Earth and that they have therefore been instilled with a residual idea in their subconscious minds that Earth was only a temporary place to live. The Atlanteans were used to a luxurious lifestyle, being pampered and cleaned up after, like having a maid. As a result, they would rely too much on technology and would lose their sense of ethics. Earth was only a temporary place to live, and they would soon have a better world to go to, and it became so entrenched in their belief system that they developed numerous religions based on one of Atlantis' flaws in that society: that they would one day move on to another world on which to live.

Next, they view plate number 98: *Destiny, Alternate Realities, and Dreams*. It relates the concept that destiny originates from higher levels of thought from alternate realities. Humans have dreams of visiting those alternate realities and experience memories in the dreams that are not true to real life. They are actually visiting these alternate realities in their mind and spirit. As those on higher levels of existence plan their lives, we at the lower levels are sometimes affected by their actions. As a result, we experience destiny.

Each human has a life force or a soul which causes the body to live and function. Many humans through their souls are linked to parallel worlds in alternate realities. The same life force can maintain multiple bodies during the same time period. Memories can sometimes be swapped back and forth through dreaming.

Rinto, Fraxino, Chispo, and the others discuss the concepts and determine that there are more reasons that we all sleep and dream than we realize.

The text also reveals some information about the race of green men on Artenia being few in number and being guardians of that world. They determine that they are meant to go to southern Zotola and search for them in the mountains.

They view another plate, this one titled: *Feelings, Personality, and Friendships*, plate number 83. The text says that human feelings are a flawless warning device in times of potential danger. As a result of the people having been instilled with the idea that Earth is only a temporary place to live, most of them will consider friendships to be of little value and importance.

Rinto points out that it is only true, seeing how many wars Earth has had, especially this century. Chris admits that most people on Earth are just not true friends. Chispo declares that he noticed that when he was in Tennessee last year, and he states that on Artenia, once a person is your friend, he stays your friend and for life. He will defend you in times of danger and will help you when asked.

People on Earth hold grudges way too easily, and they will forgive a person only if they have a use for that person. True forgiveness is completely forgetting what happened in the past and restoring the friendship 100%. .

They go to sleep for the night, and Robert dreams that Morris talks to him. Morris informs Robert that the real reason he didn't accompany them was that he received a very strong feeling that he wouldn't arrive and that some forms of communication between Earth and the Orion Belt are blocked. Morris informs Robert that he paid Tom a visit and that he has another mission for them: to go to northern Mexico and locate an Atlantean transmitter device in the mountains. It is transmitting negative vibrations and is therefore causing conflict in that region.

Morris also mentions that the Sycamore trees (*Platanus*) are a distant cousin of the Eucalyptus trees and also came to Earth with the dolphins 35 million years ago. He also recommends that Robert and his friends go find the race of green men, that it's part of their mission, and he fades from Robert's dream.

Robert wakes up in the middle of the night, wondering if Morris actually knew about the race of green men. A discussion with Tom was in order as well.

Chapter 5: HICHICERA, ZOTOLA

When everyone awakes, Robert relates to them the dream he has had of talking to Morris. Chispo mentions that they are *definitely* going to southern Zotola to search for the race of green men. Robert informs them that Morris said there is a block in place and that Tom proposes a mission of going to northern Mexico and locating the transmitter device in the mountains.

Robert and Chispo transport to Sirius B to talk with Tom. He verifies that what Morris said is indeed true. There is indeed a block to the Orion belt from Earth. Tom had met with Morris the day before, and he learned that some of Robert's friends had left the group and returned home.

Robert and Chispo, along with Tom, transport themselves to Zotola, arriving in the Zapatero's backyard. Robert introduces him to Rinto and Fraxino. Tom is most impressed by Rinto and Fraxino's Velosa cruiser craft, especially by the Ulexite main controls crystal.

Tom proceeds to tell them that the Galactic Federation has requested that the Orion Belt be added to the inner star system telephone system and that the federation knows very well that there is a civilization here on Artenia and that they are the descendants of those who fled Earth's Atlantis 12,500 years ago.

He also informs them that he is aware of the fact that Artenia has cars in agreement with federation design and that they more recently sell hydrogen fuel at their fuel stations, all under contract and agreement with the intergalactic fuel company called Exxoll.

He also tells them that there were 12 crystal transmitter devices installed at strategic locations throughout planet Earth, that they were to endure for 500 years and keep the 400 or so Earthlings who stayed behind from having access to those who fled. However, one of them got tampered with and has endured far longer than the agreed 500 years. It is hidden somewhere in the mountains of northern Mexico.

Tom offers a US $25,000 reward for locating it, switching it off, and possibly destroying it.

He admits that the federation had forgotten that such a block existed, but when they checked their historical files on Atlantis, they discovered that such a block was installed 12,500 years ago.

Tom informs them that Morris knows the reason why he couldn't have passed through the block to arrive with them, but that reason would wait until later. Morris knows much more than he lets on.

Chris checks to be sure he heard Tom right about the $25,000 reward, and Tom verifies. Everyone decides to be in on the project with a reward like that.

All of them drive off to southern Zotola, and Tom accompanies them to the ancient galactic dump site on the way. They briefly show him where they found the crate of holographic plates. They carry Tom a little ways further south on the highway where they turn him loose. He disappears behind some shrubs and teleports himself back to Sirius B.

Rinto drives them to Hichicera over a period of two days. They cross several desert valleys, mountain ranges, and some towns, as well. They drive through Efforestow and then Harkelrhodes, where they refuel with hydrogen at an Exxoll station. A man is on foot offering to sell crystal display cabinets, and Fraxino buys all three of them with enthusiasm. He gives one to Robert and says the other one is for Tom.

They cross the Colerene Mountains and enter the green coastal plains stretching to the west coast of Zotola. Later, they arrive at the coast town of Lominac. They have quick look at the town and have some fish and chips for supper.

Rinto drives them a little further south along the coast and turns left and finds a place to camp on a remote gravel road. They set up camp, and once it becomes dark, they can see the night sky much more clearly than they could in Zantaayer. Chispo points out the two nearby stars of Al Nilam, 3.2 light years away, and Mintaka, 5.8 light years away.

They continue to talk about things, and Chispo relates a frightening story about how he walked in on a convenience store robbery when he was staying on Earth last year!

The next day, they continue the trip in Rinto and Fraxino's vehicle-craft. They pass through several more towns and cross several mountain ranges, the last one being the Cloerinne Mountain range. They can now see the Zuehl Sea on the southern coast of Zotola.

In the evening, they pull into the town of Hichicera. The town is semitropical, and enjoys warm, steady temperatures year round.

Rinto, Fraxino, and Chispo inquire at several shops about the mountains. At one of the shops, Chispo casually asks if they know of an endemic race of people living in the mountains, and they send them up the street to a man who goes every other month and trades with them.

While going up the street, Chispo suddenly notices a *privately owned* Skiivona Zetna. It's very rare to see one that is privately owned. Those cars are very quick. It is the only type of car used by Zotola's highway police, nicknamed the *Zetna Force*.

They continue walking up the street and arrive at the shop where they meet Doulos, who happens to be going into the mountains tomorrow. They talk it over and arrange to meet in the morning.

The next day, Doulos takes them into the Cloerinne Mountains on a three day hike, camping at the crest of the mountains the first night and along the banks of the Makeeseldruff River the second night. There are Hemlocks, Acacias, Southern Beeches, Poplars, and other trees growing.

The third day, they have to climb up through the steep, narrow, and treacherous Makeeseldruff Gully, and they arrive at the meadow where they live.

Chapter 6: THE ATASCOSA

They are known as the Atascosa people. There are around 450 altogether, and they live in a meadow tucked between tall mountain ranges on both sides. Their small stone houses are tucked into the forested slopes on both sides of the meadow.

They do indeed have a green tinge to their skin, a genetic trait that is a remnant from bygone days many millions of years ago. The genetic traits of trees were combined with the genes of their long ago ancestors so that they would be able to manufacture food by photosynthesis, which would be useful in times of possible food shortage crises in the future. Though most of them died, there were a few who successfully accommodated the photosynthetic genes and furthered the new race of humans. As a result, they were environmentally conscious and appreciating of nature, and since ancient times, they have made their home along the banks of the Makeeseldruff River in this meadow.

Doulos takes them to the leader of the Atascosa people. His name is Zocanto, and he welcomes them into his home. They meet his wife Cawrenfra and their two children: Zahiyo and Govianna. They are in the process of learning the worldwide language of Artenian.

Doulos explains to Zocanto why he has brought his new friends with him, and after relating the stories of their adventures, Zocanto walks over to a shelf and brings an object back over to Robert. It's a crystal, and it has a mountain scene within it. It's just like the one Robert had seen in his mind when Chispo had taken them on a tour of the campus of the University of Zotola! Robert is really surprised, and he begins to ask how Zocanto knows.

The crystal had been brought to them several thousand years ago by a visitor from another part of Zotola, and it is said to have come from Atlantis. Chispo reads the crystal and telepathically receives two words: *Chiquihuitillos*, and *atasco*. There is a coincidence concerning the word *atasco*, and they realize that the origin of some words goes back further than is realized and that they have hidden meaning.

Zocanto is impressed by their abilities of discernment and says that they are the chosen seven to solve the problem of the transmitter device in Mexico. He also says they are better telepathic receivers than they realize.

Zahiyo and Govianna take them on a tour of the whole meadow. They visit terraced gardens, see the source of the Makeeseldruff River, and visit the forest of Hemlocks, Cedars, and Pines.

The next day, Zahiyo and Govianna take them to the market center. There they meet a young fellow named Orolizo who expresses interest in their mission and invites them to his house.

For the next several hours, Zahiyo and Govianna take them on a hike along the Base Cliff Trail which runs along the upper section of the forest at the foot of the mountains.

They arrive at Orolizo's house, and Orolizo happily greets them. He eagerly talks with them and informs them that he has been having disturbing dreams about a troubled young fellow who lives in a town in northern Mexico. Orolizo also has a quartz crystal ball to send to what he calls his soul link in Mexico, and he asks Chispo if he would take it to him. He is sure Chispo or someone in their group will instinctively know who he is.

They carry on chatting and visiting for several hours. Meanwhile, Steven has taken notice of Orolizo's sister, Lumela, who he can't take his eyes off of. She, Govianna, and Zahiyo have been off in another part of the room chatting.

They return to Zocanto's house, and it is soon revealed to everyone that Steven has fallen lovesick for Lumela. Orolizo comes over, and Steven is offered a 30-day program to stay with Orolizo's family and learn the way of life of the Atascosa. Steven is hesitant, but with the thoughts of Lumela's perfect beauty, he can't resist. He says goodbye to the group, and Orolizo takes him home. Robert and his friends are somewhat surprised and taken aback by the suddenness of it all.

That night, it storms and rains. In the morning, the Makeeseldruff River is up, and the storm is already passed. Steven arrives with a look of terror on his face, and he is really flustered! He declares that he is no longer staying, that he is coming with them. They ask him what is wrong, and he tells them he had a very disturbing dream of being cornered by a mean looking Mexican who was very angry and wanted to kill him. He had gotten up and left Orolizo's house as a result, and his feelings of attraction for Lumela have vanished.

The others ask Steven what he can remember about what the guy looked like, and they determine that he is likely Orolizo's soul link.

Orolizo shows up and expresses concern for Steven, and Chispo tells him what happened. Orolizo also hands Chispo a note to hand to his soul link once they find him in Mexico.

With that done, Zocanto and Cawrenfra wish Doulos and his new friends well, and they begin the three-day walk back to Hichicera. The Makeeseldruff River is really up, and the descent through the gorge is really treacherous.

Two days later, they arrive in Hichicera, and they eat supper with Doulos and his wife Clarinda.

They wish them well. Rinto drives them back to Zantaayer by a much quicker method. They *fly* home. As they gain altitude, they crest the Cloerinne Mountains and soon see the Makeeseldruff River valley and the meadow where the Atascosa people live.

In three hours, Rinto lands the craft on the gravel road of the western ridge of the Ciruclar Mountains, and he drives them down the mountainous road, making the descent into Zantaayer. Through the trees, they can see the lights of the city in the twilight.

Chapter 7: MEXICO, THE ANCIENT PAINTINGS

They arrive at the Zapateros, and Glecko greets them. Rinto and Fraxino tell their father all about their trip, and Chispo has his input as well.

Chispo's mother comes to the door for her son. She meets everyone and introduces herself as Vironga Colancha-Pachanga. She takes him home and tells him there are some chores to do.

It's not much longer before they spread out their bedrolls and go to sleep for the night.

The next morning, Rinto and Fraxino go through their rock and crystal collection and prepare a briefcase of certain crystals they are going to carry to Mexico. Among them are orange Calcite and a beautiful speciman of Purple Rainbow Fluorite.

Chispo has been doing chores in his backyard, and Fraxino sends Robert over there for the two crystals they brought back from the Atascosa people.

Rinto switches on the crystal base computer, and with everyone else looking on, he reads the two crystals. The crystal intended for Orolizo's soul link gives a read error, and they realize it has a telepathic lock on it. They look at the crystal with the mountain scene within it, and they receive images of some ancient paintings in Mexico. The crystal has provided the right avenues so that the crystal base computer can literally access the information and latch the data from the ether. The mountain scene crystal is connected straight to the location where the information is recorded in the rocks and the ether around them at the site of the ancient paintings.

Rinto decides not to look at any of the holographic plates for now, since he is anxious to go ahead and leave to Mexico.

They prepare food and water, load the vehicle-craft, and Fraxino drives them up to the mountain ridge. From there they become airborne, and as they pick up speed, they briefly feel the forcefield accompanied by a faint green glow overtake them, and they soon find themselves flying around 5,000 meters above a desert valley in northern Mexico. It is the crack of dawn there, and they are approaching the double mesa where the ancient paintings are.

Fraxino makes a rough landing on a narrow dirt lane, and Rinto now drives them to the double mesa. They park and climb the steep hillside, reaching the cliffs, and they see all the different paintings.

On the side walls of the cliffs, there are drawings of what appear to be people, tools, plantlife, animal representations, suns, moons, and even more exotic things like concentric circles, chains of diamond-shaped cross hatched squares, spacecrafts, other vehicles, and more. Most of them are painted with red and orange colors.

As they move from one wall to another on a narrow path, they have to pick their way around Cactus and Yucca-like plants, including Lechuguilla, Zotól, and other thorny shrubs.

They comment and make remarks about the interesting paintings. There are three basic areas of the paintings, and they comment that one of the drawings looks like a multistage rocket. Another looks somewhat like electrical circuitry or circuit boards. Robert notices a drawing of seven chains of cross-hatched diamonds and points it out to Chispo.

As Chispo looks at it, Andrew suggests counting the diamonds, and Chispo counts 37.5 of them. Rinto points out that if he takes out the decimal, the number is the same as the last three digits of his phone number. Chispo is very surprised and comments that it is far out!

Robert points out that the number of columns are the same as the number in their group: seven.

Chispo is beside himself, and he declares that the depiction was drawn so that one day, the seven of them would come and see it. The depiction has plenty of hidden meaning to it because they realize even more coincidences about it and some other drawings right around it. There is a drawing of a dolphin nearby and also a drawing of a sun with flames above it. They think it may represent a dying sun, and they recall that Morris had told them that Delikadove, the old home world of the dolphins, got destroyed 35 million years ago. There is more still, as Robert points to an image of what looks like a Eucalyptus twig right above the drawing of the dolphin. They remember that the Eucalyptus trees came with the dolphins when they arrived to Earth 35 million years ago. They determine that somebody from Atlantis knew all of this, and that certain information in these depictions was intended only for the seven of them, when they would come along thousands of years later.

They move on to a third section of drawings and see a mountain scene with a beam or ray taking off from the second peak. Rinto takes out the mountain scene crystal from Zocanto, and it is a perfect match with the mountain range west of them.

They leave the paintings and walk back to the vehicle-craft. They definitely think the paintings are 12,000 years old, drawn after the Atlanteans fled from Earth.

Rinto flies them to the summit of the second peak west of the desert valley, and they look for evidence of spacecraft landings, thinking that it was an ancient landing pad.

Next, Rinto flies them over to the mountain range east of the desert valley, and when they fly over the ridge top, they can see a town way below them to the east. In alarm, for fear of being seen by some of the residents, Rinto quickly turns around and returns to the west side of the mountain range. He flies them to a canyon opening to the north, and brings it in for a landing.

As they follow a rough gravel road downhill, they see a beautiful spring and pond on their left. It is situated in a beautiful woods of Anaqua, Ash, Mesquite, and Sycamore trees. They stop for a swim and end up camping for the night. The place is known as the Ojo del Agua.

Later, a rancher comes by in his old pickup truck and talks Spanish with Andrew and Robert.

The next morning, Chispo drives them to Bustamante on a one-lane gravel road for ten kilometers, and they enter the northwest side of Bustamante, Nuevo León.

Chapter 8: BUSTAMANTE, NUEVO LEON

The road entering town turns out to be the main street through town, Calle Mier. Bustamante has a population of around 3,000 residents, and most of them are lifetime natives. The whole town in some ways is like a large family with everyone connected to everyone else in some way. There are no banks, no law offices, no fast-food restaurants, no convenience stores, and no traffic lights. There is not even a fuel station, the nearest one being a Pemex station ten kilometers away.

Bustamante is situated in a grove or oasis of mostly Pecan trees and is at the foot of the mountains, the main feature being the Lion's Head Mountain, locally called Cabeza de León, elevation 1,860 meters.

Chispo turns right on a street named Escobedo, and they pull up in front of a bakery. They are the Casso family, and they sell various baked breads. As they step out of the vehicle, they inquire about the types.

At that time, the youngest son, Paco, who is their age, sees them and expresses quite a bit of surprise at the vehicle-craft. He talks with them, and he gives them a tour of the bakery and of his carpentry business making chairs. They tell Paco they have come to Mexico in an American futuristic prototype vehicle and that they had seen the ancient paintings yesterday. Paco takes them to his father who tells them stories of giants who had lived in the region thousands of years ago. He also tells them other ancient legends.

Paco's workers arrive, and one of them is named Roel. Robert brings up that they need a guide while they are in Mexico, and Paco offers them to hire Roel since the carpentry business is a little slow at the moment. Paco leaves them to it, as he has to go to Sabinas Hidalgo to run errands.

Roel is age 16 and is tall and slender for a Mexican. He has a look of irresistible curiosity on his face. He feels blessed to have been released of his hard work and is now eager to begin his new job as a tourist guide. With a smile on his face, he asks them to show him their vehicle, and they walk out front on the street and show it to him. He finds it interesting.

He directs them to Sabastian Xavier, an investigator of odd phenomena, and they chat with him about the ancient paintings and that their age is actually 12,500 years instead of 2,500. Roel now finds out that three of them: Rinto, Fraxino, and Chispo are from another star system.

Next, Roel directs them to the plaza, and Rinto circles it several times at Roel's request. He waves and whistles at his friends. On the third round, a policeman waves them over, and Roel talks to him. His name is Jorge, and he is a personal friend of Roel's. After they chat and even though Roel tells him the vehicle is from another world, Jorge waves them on and tells them to go ahead.

They visit the church on the other side of the plaza, and Roel tells them about the 300-year-old mannequin of Jesus, and that every August 6th, there is a big carnival in Bustamante, and they march around the town's streets with the statue. Bustamante used to be called Boca de Leones (Mouth of the Lions) in those days, then San Miguel de Aguayo, and later came to be called Bustamante, being named after one of Mexico's presidents, Gral. Anastasio Bustamante of the mid 1800's.

Next, they walk over to a corner store, and they meet the owners, Chilo and Mina Cantu. Roel buys a snack and a Jumex drink. Robert notices a sign hanging in the back of the store, and it reads: *No fio porque cobrar es un lío, y el negocio es mío.* (I don't sell on credit because charging is a complicated matter, and the place of business is mine.) Why is there such mistrust?

Roel suggests that they go fetch his brother, Rudy, age 15, and they go to Felipe Hernandez' carpentry business where Rudy works. They meet and chat with Felipe, and Rudy accompanies them to their home where they meet Roel and Rudy's family. María is the mother, and there are two daughters: Nora and Idalia, ages 11 and 6. María serves everyone lunch.

Rudy is also tall and slender for a Mexican, not quite as tall as Roel. He has the face of a genuine friend, and they would soon find that to be the truth. Both Roel and Rudy attend the prepa in Sabinas Hidalgo, and they are out for summer vacation.

For the afternoon, they decide to go to the caves up in the mountains. Chispo does the driving. On the way, soon after leavinng, they stop at a street corner at Roel's request so he can chat with two friends of his: Alvaro and Pegaso.

Steven suddenly expresses a lot of worry because he recognizes Pegaso as the mean, angry Mexican fellow who he had seen in the disturbing dream when he spent the night with Orolizo. Chispo and the others calm him down and reassure him that they will protect him if necessary.

Suddenly, a rush of thoughts enter Chispo's mind in a split second. They came from Rudy. Chispo reacts with surprise and suddenly realizes he can speak Spanish. The others are surprised, and they realize that Rudy unknowingly telepathically gave Chispo the whole Spanish language!

Roel finishes talking to his friends and enters the vehicle-craft again. Chispo drives everyone to the cave, and they hike up the trail for 45 minutes. They meet Ramiro Gomez, the cave guide, and he charges a small admission and takes everyone inside. They are amazed at the size of the cave, one of the largest in the world. It had been discovered by a native of Bustamante in the early part of the century while he was up in the mountains manning his goats.

Ramiro gives them a tour of the three main sections, taking over an hour. They leave the cave and descend the mountain to the cono with him. He rides with them back to town in the vehicle-craft, and they stop by his uncle-in-law's house and meet Daniel Mata.

Daniel is very interested in the ancient paintings, and he chats with them about them. He also has quite a yard with a collection of native plants from the whole region.

They return to Roel and Rudy's house and chat for a while. They decide to return to the mountains tomorrow, this time to camp and also look for the transmitter device. Rudy decides to join in on all their adventures and also becomes their guide alongside Roel.

Later, they go over to the house where Roel's friend Pegaso lives, and they meet his whole family. Chispo, Steven, and Chris take a liking to him, and they decide to stay over at Pegaso's house. Steven removes his fear and puts himself at ease. Pegaso expresses interest in their vehicle-craft, and Roel admits to him that three of them are from another star system.

Chispo reads the sign on the front of Pegaso's family's house, and it says: *Bienvenidos a la casa Orolizo-Ziscaya*. Chispo is amazed and so are the others, and they now have definite proof that Pegaso is indeed Orolizo's soul link, especially since his last name is the same. They visit, and they meet Pegaso's sisters: Lumita and Mena. They are very pretty.

The others return to Roel and Rudy's house and eat supper, and then they return to Pegaso's house, and all of them pile into the vehicle-craft. They stop by Alvaro's house and pick him up also, and they go over to Villaldama to cruise the town a while, stop and walk the plaza, chat with the girls, and briefly visit the dance.

They return to Bustamante and go to sleep. Roel and Rudy's father arrives around 1 AM from the cantina (bar) where he has been playing pool and cards with his buddies. He sleeps in.

The next morning, they prepare their backpacks and food, and they stop by Pegaso's house for Chispo, Steven, and Chris. Pegaso soon leaves to help his father. Pegaso's mother explains that he is not the mountain hiking type. She chats with them. They feel blessed to have Roel and Rudy for their guides because they do indeed have an interest in hiking in the mountains.

Rinto drives them to the cono where they park the vehicle-craft and take some crystals.

Chapter 9: THE SEARCH IN THE MOUNTAINS

They ascend the trail, passing by the cave again, and they continue, passing by a long rock cliff on their left. The trail winds its way into a forested gully where they stop to eat lunch.

They are compelled to look upward at a free standing rock cliff. It draws their attention.

After lunch, they continue as the trail leaves the gully. In one place, they have to climb a steep section and use a rope. They follow the trail up to the main forested ridge of Oak and Hickory trees, and they hike through this moderate forest for the next half hour until they arrive at a grassy saddle where they come to a major dropoff to the west. It must be 300 meters to the bottom!

They set up camp and leave Chris there, and the others continue ascending to the top of a limestone ridge where Cypress shrubs and scrub Oaks grow.

While Rinto and Fraxino take readings with their crystals, Roel and Rudy and the others look around and explore. Suddenly, by instinct, Roel plunges his hand down a rock crevice and pulls up a bronze metal tablet. He calls Chispo over, and he and the others are amazed. As Chispo brushes the loose dirt off of it, he is amazed even further to see that it is written in Atlantean hieroglyphic script. It also has a depiction. It is a memorial marker to a leader of the group that stayed behind. His name was Bocaleo, and he would be missed.

They return to camp and realize that his name so closely matches the name Boca de Leones, which is what Bustamante used to be called in the old days.

They camp for the night in the grassy saddle, and Roel and Rudy relate to them stories about Bustamante, including some conflicts and danger. They relate a story about a retired American school teacher who came to Bustamante to stay a few years ago for the winter. In addition to rejecting her former student friend after he had immensely helped her out by bringing two trailer cargos to her cousins, she resorted to defaming certain individuals in the town, and they freaked out and eliminated her. Her husband loaded his truck and fled town in a hurry, scared to death!

They also relate a story about how one family went hysterical and used the police to run off a young American fellow for having unintentionally done something a little wrong. They comment how insane that was and blame the transmitter device for having caused it.

Roel and Rudy also tell them that they were born and raised near Pinos, Zacatecas. They haven't been back there for 8 years, and they miss their grandparents and cousins.

They also tell them that their house is up for sale for $8,000, and the Cantu family owns it.

After camping for the night, they hike back down the mountain the same way they came up, and they talk about more plans about how to locate and pinpoint the transmitter device.

They return to Bustamante by the afternoon, and Roel and Rudy enjoy telling their mother hair raising, exaggerated stories about their hiking and camping trip into the mountains. Roel shows her the bronze plaque he found, and he stores it in a safe place in the house. They take a nap.

Chapter 10: HIDDEN DANGER

Pegaso comes over, and everyone goes over to the molino (swimming pool). They meet Hector and Pablo Cizneros, and Robert also meets and talks to Victor. He warns Robert of Pegaso, saying that he gets angry very easily and in a hurry. Robert goes over to Chispo and calls him over to the side to tell him. Chispo reassures Robert that he can overpower Pegaso if necessary.

They return to Roel and Rudy's house, and Chispo, Steven, and Chris return to Pegaso's house, Everyone gets cleaned up and ready for the Saturday night activities, the dance.

They pass by Pegaso's house, and the others join them. Chispo has discovered another coincidence. His phone number is the same as Pegaso's: 60375. He tells everyone.

They meet Alvaro in the plaza by the dance hall. Some of them enter, and Rudy, Chispo, Alvaro, Rinto, and Robert walk over to the main plaza by the church. Rudy and Alvaro see some friends of theirs and chat with them.

Robert sees Victor with some friends of his, and he introduces Chispo and Rinto to them. One of the friends, Luis, asks Chispo how he likes the pretty women in the town. He asks him what he thinks of Pegaso's sisters. Chispo casually answers that Lumita is pretty and would please him for a girlfriend. Luis reacts with laughter and jokes with him that Chispo and Pegaso could be brothers-in-law. They all start laughing and have a good hearty laugh about the whole idea.

Then Rinto and Chispo take Victor and his friends to the vehicle-craft and give them a ride around Bustamante. They enjoy it and thank them.

Afterwards, Rinto, Robert, and Chispo return to Roel and Rudy's and Pegaso's houses to go to sleep for the night. They don't attend the dance. Rudy and Alvaro do enter the dance. They and the others arrive around 2 AM and sleep late Sunday morning.

Around mid day Sunday, they decide to go to Sabinas Hidalgo to visit the flea market and other stores. They stop by Pegaso's house for Chispo, Chris, and Steven. Pegaso does not accompany them, and Chispo tells them that Pegaso does not appear very happy.

On the way, Chispo asks Roel what is wrong with Pegaso, and Roel says not to worry about it. They stop at a small market in Villaldama, and then they drive to Sabinas Hidalgo. They eat lunch, visit the stores, the flea market, a large supermarket called Garza Morton, and return to Bustamante. They are so appreciating of their new friends in Bustamante and how Roel and Rudy's family and Pegaso's family are so friendly and hospitable.

They let Chispo, Steven, and Chris off at Pegaso's house, and the others return to Roel and Rudy's house. Around 20 minutes later as they are eating supper, Chispo, followed by Steven and Chris, suddenly walk in and plop down their backpacks. Rudy goes into the front room to check to see what is the matter.

Chispo relates a horrifying story that Pegaso attacked him and went round and round with him and also Steven! Chispo had to sock Pegaso in the stomach to save himself, and he also put Pegaso unconscious by squeezing his shoulder.

Roel and Rudy are very much surprised, and Roel, Rinto, Fraxino, Andrew, and Robert go over to the Orolizos to see if they can fix the problem and get Pegaso to apologize to Chispo. Rinto and Fraxino explain the culture differences, and Roel orders Pegaso to apologize to Chispo. It's no use. Pegaso is so stubborn as a mule, and he cannot admit that he did wrong. Pegaso had gotten so angry at Chispo because he had casually said that his sister Lumita was pretty and would please him for a girlfriend. Roel says he no longer feels comfortable with Pegaso, and they all leave.

All of them stay at Roel and Rudy's house for the remainder of their stay in Bustamante. While they had talked to Pegaso, Rudy had been talking to Chispo about Pegaso and culture differences.

For Chispo, what hurt him the most was that he had been tricked. He had given Pegaso his true friendship. Short term friendships were just not a usual practice back in his homeland of Zotola.

They all go to sleep for the night with plans to climb the Lion's Head Mountain tomorrow.

Chapter 11: THE LION'S HEAD

Roel and Rudy get up at 5:30 AM, and the others also get up. It is still dark outside. They prepare their packs and food for the long day hike. Chispo and Steven have trouble getting up after their disturbing evening because of what happened with Pegaso.

They leave the house not long after 6 AM, and they spend the whole morning climbing the mountain slope, following the left ridge of the Lion's Head Mountain to the ridge on the right hand side of the summit. They turn left and follow the narrow ridge of limestone bedrock to the summit, making a scramble to the flat table at the top. A few Cypress shrubs also grow up there.

While they eat lunch, Rinto and Fraxino take readings with their crystals, feel confident with their data, and they feel sure the crystal transmitter device is on the free standing rock wall that they had all looked up at while they ate lunch the other day when they went camping in the grassy saddle to the south of here.

Roel telepathically hears two friends of his making plans to throw a firecracker. They are Pegaso and a friend of his, Beto. Roel angrily declares that Pegaso is crazy and wonders why he cannot admit that he did wrong and apologize.

Just as they are packing to leave, they hear a whirring sound, and they see a pink glow. A person makes his appearance. It is Morris, and Roel and Rudy are very surprised, not having seen anyone arriving by such a method before! Everyone is surprised to see Morris suddenly show up.

Morris has been doing dolphin research on their old home world of Delikadove. He has arrived to warn them of some danger awaiting them in Bustamante, and he also brings it to Rinto and Fraxino's attention that there is a second transmitter in the next range to the west. He points at Roel and tells them to take that fellow with them, that he will find it straight away. Rinto and Fraxino realize they have overlooked that possibility. Morris wishes everyone well and leaves. Rinto and Fraxino recheck their readings and sure enough, find another pulse from the next range over. They feel slightly embarrassed, but they are thankful at the same time.

They descend the mountain, arriving in Bustamante 6 hours later, just before dark. Nora and Idalia are in the street, and they greet them as they arrive.

Antonio also talks to everyone and is impressed by all they have done. María serves them supper. Some neighbors also come over to chat, after which they go to sleep. They are tired after the long day's hike.

At 11 PM, everyone is suddenly awakened by a most disturbing POW! A firecracker has been thrown in the kitchen through the window, and everyone gets up to investigate. Everyone is startled. Rinto, Fraxino, and Chispo are worried about the vehicle-craft, and they run outside to investigate. They are relieved to see it undamaged.

Roel suspects that the culprits are Pegaso and Beto, and María walks to the police station to report them. Roel accompanies her. The police soon round up Pegaso and Beto, and they haul them over to the scene and match up boot and shoe prints. They are caught! The police put them in jail for three days and charge them a fine.

Everyone eventually gets back to sleep.

The next morning, Roel and Rudy suggest that they leave Bustamante, and they also offer to come with them and continue being their guides. Their mother suggests that they go visit their homeland in Zacatecas, and after talking it over, they decide to go there.

Rinto is more hesitant, not knowing where to get hydrogen fuel, but Chispo explains that it is the least they can do for Roel and Rudy after their having been so kind to be their guides and friends, as well. They all agree.

They pack their things, and by late morning, Chispo drives them to the police station to secure a travel permit. Then they enter the canyon, stopping by the Ojo del Agua where some of them go swimming.

Once they leave the Ojo del Agua, Rinto does the driving and puts the craft in flying mode. They fly over to the mesa wall paintings and look at them, after which they fly over to the mountain range on the west side of the desert valley where they land on the top of the flat table of limestone.

Roel so casually finds the crystal transmitter device and right away, just like Morris had predicted. Rinto flies them over to the other mountain range near Bustamante, and Roel quickly finds the other transmitter on a ledge below the free standing rock wall, which is right where Rinto and Fraxino suspected it was.

Next, they take off flying, and in a matter of a few hours they reach Zacatecas.

Chapter 12: ZACATECAS

On the way, they touch down on the highway between Saltillo and Zacatecas, and they are surprised at how similar it is to the highway and scenery south of Zantaayer.

Zacatecas is in the central Mexican highlands, and most of the scenery is desert-like with large Palma Real trees very similar to Joshua Trees. There are also some large, tree size Nopal plants.

They later arrive and touch down just north of Pinos, Zacatecas, and they drive into town. Roel asks where his uncle Antonio lives, and they go to his house and meet his family. They are glad to see them. His wife is Eustolia, and their two children are Joel and Malena.

Antonio sets them up with a place to stay across the road where his brother-in-law lives. There are beds for everyone. They take a nap, then eat supper with them, visit for a while, and then go back to sleep since they had done a lot of activities the previous few days.

The next day, Chispo drives them to the town of San Miguel, and they visit Roel and Rudy's grandparents on their ranch. Their oldest son still lives there and farms it. They eat lunch and have a look around the place, visit with them, and then they leave to visit others relatives in San Miguel. There Roel meets a beautiful cousin named Camila.

As they visit, Roel takes to her, and he and she talk. Feelings of excitement run through him.

On the way back to Pinos, Roel feels sad to be separated from her.

The next morning, they prepare to leave and return to Zotola. Roel surprises everyone by suddenly backing out and staying. The others cannot talk him into continuing with them. Though Roel doesn't admit it, he does not want to return to Bustamante for at least a month because he is afraid of what Pegaso and Beto might do to him after having been arrested.

Rudy decides to continue with them, and they leave Pinos. Roel is sad to see them go, and Eustolia comforts him. Rudy enjoys his new friends. Rinto drives them out of town and puts the craft in flying mode. The forcefield soon takes them over.

Chapter 13: RETURN TO ZOTOLA

Before they totally realize it, they are flying high above the desert valley south of Zantaayer's Ciruclar Mountains. It is the crack of dawn, and Rudy comments with surprise at the sky being more green than Earth's.

They touch down on the highway, drive over the Ciruclar Mountains, and as they descend the highway into Zantaayer, Rudy finds it very familiar, and he feels like he has been there before. Perhaps his soul is from Zotola. They return to the Zapateros.

Glecko greets them and notices they have a new friend, Rudy. Everyone tells Glecko all about their adventures, including the hair raising stories, like Pegaso getting so angry at Chispo for saying that his sister was pretty, the firecracker incident, and the arrest.

Rinto and Fraxino, along with the others, go to the crystal base computer and begin analyzing the data they have collected with their crystals.

One of the crystals has recorded a story about the renegades from the days of Atlantis. One of the renegades was named Cobra Ressmahlo, and he was a trouble maker who had set into motion numerous quantum energy systems which caused adverse effects and human conflicts in Atlantean society. It says that he would be remembered in subtle ways for many millennia to come.

Everyone at first thinks the story is totally irrelevant, and they don't know what quantum energy systems are. They scan the holographic plates index, and sure enough there is a plate pertaining to the subject. Plate number 80, *Living Quantum Energy Systems and Reality*.

According to the narrative of the plate, there is a most interesting life force that has been discovered, that of living quantum energy systems, and they are self-feeding and can cause many synchronicities in life. They can be set up in a good way and can protect an individual and bring good luck, or they can be set up in a bad way and bring bad luck to a person.

It also says the primary key to discovering the aspects to Atlantean society would be through realization thousands of years in the future by certain individuals of synchronicities that will bring certain people together and discover and unravel the subtle information left behind.

They all realize that they had certainly done that by investigating the ancient paintings.

They figure out the name Cobra Ressmahlo. Andrew brings it to their attention that the name is very similar to the Spanish words *Cobrar es malo*, which means *To charge is bad*. Chispo somehow figures it out and realizes that each time people in Mexico charge someone else money, they unconsciously think of the Atlantean trouble making renegade and get angry as a result. Rudy verifies that is true in Mexico and that there is an old saying that says if you want to lose a friend, charge him money. Robert remembers the sign he saw in the Cantu's store, *No fio porque cobrar es un lío*, and he now realizes why it was put there.

They view another holographic plate, this one plate number 97: *Mysterious Rejections: Dreams vs. Reality*.

Top Atlantean psychoanalysts have arrived at the most up-to-date theory about the most annoying aspect of mysterious rejections and why they occur. People who are very good friends sometimes reject certain friends for seemingly no apparent reason. The holographic plate relates the concept of alternate realities and how good friends can be totally congenial in this world's reality, but in the alternate reality, they may have had a fight. Sometimes the non-peaceful patterns can bleed over to this reality and cause them to reject one another.

Chispo thinks that's what likely happened with Pegaso. Plus they all remember Roel and Rudy's story about the retired American school teacher and how she had suddenly rejected her former student friend. They realize she had resonated very strongly to the crystal transmitter device.

They analyze more data from the crystals, and they find out more about the block that had been set in place by the Atlanteans to keep the 400 or so people who stayed behind on Earth from contacting them. The blocking force was to endure for 500 years. 200 years after they had fled, an expedition team went to the northern Mexico desert valley to find the legendary crystals. They soon realized they had made a major mistake because when they tampered with them, they caused the transmitters to run indefinitely, and any negative quantum energy systems were amplified and kept alive as a result.

Another crystal gives them some coordinate data. Rinto and Fraxino start to feel the tension of the project at hand, and Rinto asks Chispo if he and the others can do some other activities for the next several days.

Chispo drives Andrew, Chris, Robert, Rudy, and Steven to Caloma, a region north of Zotola. His Velva Dibe car can't fly, like Rinto and Fraxino's. It takes them all day to get there. Chispo's parents are from there, a place called the Vovvitlet Valley situated at the base of the Urlachia Mountains. The city is called Zwever.

Chispo crests the mountains on the highway approaching Zwever, and he drives them down into the city. It is already near midnight when they arrive and pull up to his aunt Esalina's house. Her son Cliss, who is Chispo's age, happily greets them and welcomes them inside. His aunt soon arrives, having been out shopping, and they also happily greet each other.

They stay overnight, and the next morning they are very impressed by the scenery of the surrounding mountains. The climate is indeed cooler than down south in Zotola.

Chispo drives them into Zwever's central district where they tour different sites and shop at the flea markets. Some of them buy some souvenirs. Chispo treats them to lunch and then takes them to a movie.

It is called *The Chill of the Vovvitlet*, and it is about an expedition team who climbs the highest peak in the region, Horcones Peak, and they are confronted with ghostly apparitions. The movie really puts chills down their backs.

They return to Esalina's house and visit. Everyone realizes that the planet of Artenia has no radio nor television. Some of the native races of humans and also the dolphins and whales were annoyed by the transmissions, and the idea of electromagnetic waves had to be abandoned.

The next day, they go hiking in the Urlachia Mountains along the Wyndham Way. The forest scenery and alpine meadows are beautiful.

They return to Esalina's house and spend the afternoon in Zwever's central district where Andrew, Robert, and Rudy buy more souvenirs.

They spend the night, and the next day they return to Zantaayer, taking all day to drive there. Robert and Rudy help with the driving. They arrive at dark, and they spend the night at the Zapateros.

The next morning, Rinto and Fraxino arrive from the mountain cave where they have been growing the crystal apparatus to take to Mexico with them. Everyone marvels at the setup and is impressed. Glecko praises his sons for their abilities, and Sosta admits likewise. The crystal setup consists of Kaolinite, 4 red phantom crystals, Ruby, and some pieces of Kanágran, a green crystal found on Artenia but not on Earth.

They prepare to leave, say goodbye to Glecko and Sosta, and Rinto drives them to the mountains on the western side of Zantaayer, drives up the forested gravel road, leaves the ground, and they teleport back to Mexico.

Chapter 14: SOLUTION FROM THE MOUNTAINS

They make their appearance over the desert valley and drive to Bustamante via the Ojo del Agua. It is Monday, July 22, and it is mid afternoon. The weather is hot and sunny as usual.

When they arrive at Roel and Rudy's house, María greets them and tells them that Roel had called from Zacatecas. He had told her that the others had gone to visit another star system. María also tells them that Roel said he didn't want to continue with them because he thought they were gay. Rudy responds by insisting they are not gay, and he tells her the real reason: that Roel didn't want to return to Bustamante because he was afraid of Pegaso. No matter what, María is stuck on the idea of their being gay, and she mandates Rudy to no longer accompany them. Rudy defends his friends and again insists they are not gay. He says that he is obligated to be his friends' guide, and he will not abandon them like Roel did. He has to disobey his mother and leaves with them.

They leave Bustamante, but not without encountering Pegaso and Beto in the street. They are mocking them, showing them the hand sign for gay. Rinto causes the craft to momentarily leave the ground, and they pass over their heads. Rinto then drives them into the canyon where he next flies them over to the mountain ridge west of the double mesa.

There Robert and Chispo rappel down to the ledge where one of the crystal transmitters is sitting. It is a dodecahedron, and its appearance is impressive. They place a receiver crystal next to it. Next, they fly over to the other mountain range and do the same, followed by flying to the ridge top where they place their Kaolinite crystal setup.

They fly over to the summit of the Lion's Head Mountain and wait for dark. At that time, Rinto and Fraxino telepathically send the trigger signals and successfully switch off the transmitters.

Then a big surprise comes. White flashes of light begin, and everyone immediately runs for cover the best they can. Chris stumbles and falls. Flashes soon start surging all over the desert valleys. Explosions are heard. One of the last surges passes right over the Lion's Head summit and kills Chris!

When it's all over, they discover Chris. Rinto and Fraxino revive him with their crystal first aid kit. Chris is very thankful to have his life force restored.

Suddenly, Morris arrives and expresses that he is most impressed by what they have done. He says he could detect the display of energy all the way over to where he was on Delikadove, the world of the dolphins. He explains to them how well the energy systems have been neutralized and how everything will be found a lot better in Bustamante. He also explains the process and tells them what the different energy systems actually caused: the different adverse effects. Even still, people are responsible for their own actions, and they need to be careful not to revive the energy systems.

Morris transports himself away, and they camp on the summit for the night. The next morning, they return to Bustamante, first arriving at Rudy's house. María happily greets them and apologizes to them for thinking badly of them yesterday. She also asks them about the bright flashes of light and explosions that could be heard from the mountains last night.

Pegaso and Beto come over and apologize, and Pegaso apologizes to Chispo for having gotten so angry. He tells Chispo he can take his sister out on a date if he so wishes. They shake hands and become friends again.

They cruise the town in the vehicle-craft, stop by Alvaro's house, and take him with them. He apologizes for having told Pegaso what Chispo said. They visit the Cantu's store, and the *No fío porque cobrar es un lío* sign has been removed and is sitting by the trash can. They stop by the Cassos, and they buy some rocking chairs from Paco. He asks about the flashes of light and explosions that came from the mountains last night.

They return to Rudy's house. Pegaso and Beto and Alvaro go home and wish everyone well. María serves them lunch, and while they are eating, Tom and Morris arrive. They greet them, and then Tom and Morris request to talk to the seven of them and Rudy out in the vehicle-craft.

Tom rewards them US $25,000 for a job well done. He informs them that the block is indeed cleared. He has tested out gravity wave signals, and they arrived to the Orion star system perfectly. They decide to let Morris have 15% ($3,750) of it since he helped them so quickly identify where the transmitters were. Then they decide to give Rudy $100 for his being their guide, plus $8,000 so that he can buy their house. They divide the remaining amount among themselves.

Rudy is ecstatic, thanks them, and runs into the house, literally drags his parents to the vehicle-craft, and they go to the Cantu's store where Rudy and his parents buy the house. Then they return to their house, and María and Antonio proudly begin repairs on it.

Tom gets ready to leave. They give Tom one of the crystal display cabinets that they had obtained in Zotola, and he is very glad to receive it, saying it will make a nice addition to his collection, and he thanks them. He teleports away and returns to Sirius B.

The others, including Rudy, leave Bustamante with Rinto, Fraxino, and Chispo in the Velosa cruiser craft. Morris accompanies them.

They briefly view the damage the explosions had done to the ridge at the mountain top.

They fly to Zacatecas. On the way, Morris explains to them about parallel universes, that he has been visiting them, and he explains how Robert's parallel counterpart is aware of them from his level of reality. He explains how he and Chispo's parallel counterparts were only temporary friends and how the stress of life on planet Earth affected that.

They visit Pinos, and they find Roel at Antonio's house. Roel is glad to see them and greets them with a smile on his face. He apologizes to them for having backed out on them. Rudy assures Roel that all is safe in Bustamante, and they tell Roel all about what has happened. They laugh and enjoy the chat. No matter what, Roel decides to stay. He likes it in Pinos, and he has new friends.

The rest of them decide to leave and return to Zotola. Rudy accompanies them. Roel stands on the street side and waves at them as they drive away. Rinto drives them south on the highway leaving town, and he puts the craft in flying mode. As they declare that peace and friendship will prevail over northern Mexico, the forcefield accompanied by the faint green glow overtakes them.

They are off to more adventures in Zotola.

Summary and Synopsis of:
HERITAGE FINDINGS FROM ATLANTIS
written by: Robert S. Sanders, Jr., 1998-2000

How can finding five buried crates of time frozen bodies from Atlantis change the project plans of some teenagers in Alaska?

Introduction and Character Sketch

This novel is the continuation of *Mission Beyond the Ice Cave: Atlantis-Mexico-Zotola*, and is the third novel of the Galactic Salesman trilogy. Having completed their mission of eliminating the mysterious communications block in the mountains of northern Mexico, the teenagers return to Al Nitak in the Orion star system with their lively friends: Rinto, Fraxino, and Chispo in their Velosa cruiser craft. They examine more holographic plates, revisit the ancient galactic dump site, and find another bronze crate filled with . . .

Rinto, Fraxino, and Chispo are descendants of the people of Atlantis, and they live in a city called Zantaayer, Zotola, a beautiful clean city nestled within the Ciruclar Mountains. Their society is on the same level of technological advancement as their cousins on Earth. However, the air is crisp and clear because there are no fossil fuels used, since they never had a coal age.

Rinto and Fraxino Zapatero are wizards, to say the least, and they have an uncanny ability to interpret crystals, grow them, and harness their knowledge and intelligence to operate their Velosa cruiser craft and their crystal base computer system. They also have a secret lab in a cave deep within the Ciruclar Mountains.

Chispo Colancha is a lively character, always full of spark and enthusiasm, as his name suggests. He is Rinto and Fraxino's nearby neighbor and good friend, and he is involved in Rinto and Fraxino's projects, as well.

Tom, the galactic salesman, comes forth with another mission, this one the grandest of them all. He sends the teenagers to the high mountain reaches of northern Alaska where the Galactic Federation is overseeing a major 15-year galactic station project, to involve literally millions of Earth's telephone numbers, and to be built deep within Mt. Isto. By chance, they unearth five bronze crates, each containing a time frozen body . . . from Atlantis! Can they revive them?

Find out the true reasons for the galactic dump site and why the holographic plates were dumped there. Discover more revelations about trees and plants, from sacred stories, holographic plates, and the Atlanteans. Venture with them as they help Tom and his crew in building the galactic station in Alaska, what it features, from adventures, to time travel, and how it . . .

PROLOGUE

The novel begins with Tom, the galactic salesman from Sirius B. He and his friend Caymar are on the remote high mountains of northeastern Alaska. It is a bright, sunny, midsummer day, and they are choosing a site for the Galactic Federation's next assignment, to be tucked between three high, snow-covered and jagged peaks: Mt. Chamberlin, Mt. Michelson, and Mt. Isto, towering around 9,000 feet.

They are walking the mountain slopes observing the tundra laden valley way below and to the west. Tom and Caymar talk to each other in their native Sirian language, discussing possible sites for the 15-year major project of building a secret intergalactic switching station deep within the mountains, to utilize literally millions of telephone lines. One of the largest Galactic Federation projects ever, Tom and Caymar are looking forward to soon getting started.

As they discuss where to place various types of equipment, Caymar discovers a strange metal object sticking out of the ground. He and Tom unearth what is a bronze crate, and upon prying it open, discover a time frozen human body! They decide to keep it a secret from the Galactic Federation, and they quickly re-bury it.

Their next plan is to contact Morris for help.

Chapter 1: THE HOLOGRAPHIC PLATES
July 23, 1985, 4 PM

Robert and his friends: Andrew, Chris, and Steven, along with Rudy, are with Rinto and Fraxino Zapatero and Chispo in their Velosa cruiser craft. Morris is also along this time.

They are flying over the central Mexican highlands of Zacatecas, and Rinto sends his telepathic command to their on-board controls crystal. A forcefield accompanied by a faint green glow briefly overcomes them, and they find themselves flying over a desert valley of Zotola, headed north toward the city of Zantaayer surrounded by the Ciruclar Mountains. It is early morning.

Chispo, a lively character and Rinto and Fraxino's across the yard neighbor and good friend, is telling everyone about a new movie just released called *Vision from the Ciruclar.*

As they head north, Fraxino inserts a holodisk into their on-board player. Soon, some very moving pop music plays from a local group called *The Hydragyros.* As the album plays through the songs, Morris and the others are impressed and are gripped with an uncanny sense of familiarity.

Rinto steers the craft in for a landing along the gravel road running the ridge top of the Ciruclar Mountains, after which they make the winding descent through beautiful Nothofagus trees to Zantaayer in the valley below. How clear and clean the air is here in Zotola on planet Artenia, the third planet out from their star Al Nitak.

Rinto, Fraxino, and Chispo describe the technical details of their planet, size, length of days, distances, and other pertinent information. Chispo tells them again about Cresma, a heroic man who caused the arrival of over 65,000 Atlanteans 10,130 Artenian years ago.

They pull into the Zapatero's driveway and are greeted by Glecko and Sosta, Rinto and Fraxino's parents. Immediately, they describe the success they had in northern Mexico, eliminating the two dodecahedron crystal transmitters hidden in the mountains above Bustamante, Nuevo León, that were blocking communication between Earth's Sol System and Al Nitak.

Next, Rinto and Fraxino take everyone to their crystal base computer. Morris, who's here on Artenia for the first time, thanks to the clearing of the communications block, is very impressed with the computer setup, and he comments that it is more along the lines of how the dolphins do it.

They view more of their holographic plates. One of them, plate number 84, is called *Friendships and Their Own Life Force*. This plate talks about how Atlantean society has theorized that friendships have their own life force, that is, a living quantum energy system, which keeps the friendship going without much effort from the two people involved. People who are blessed with this type of friendship become very close friends. The system comes from a higher level of reality, and people of this type of friendship when they meet each other feel an immediate connection of friendship. It's as if they've known each other all their lives. Those not blessed with the friendship living quantum energy systems are usually incompatible, feeling no real friendship.

They view another plate called, *Meeting Familiar People and Acquired Nervousness*, plate number 85. This plate talks about people of the right vibrational frequencies meeting each other and finding themselves very familiar. However, since the disappearance of the Fluorite peace keeping crystal over 2,500 years ago, some of those people acquire second thoughts and begin to feel nervous for no sufficient reason. There are intelligent quantum energy systems set up by devious Atlantean scientists specifically designed to detect true potentially good friendships and sabotage them, causing the two friends to resent each other, causing alienation and grief. The friendship fails.

Robert and his friends declare that's a grim outlook on friendships.

Morris says that plate speaks the truth and comments what a shame it is that so many friendships have been lost on planet Earth due to such sabotage.

They view plate number 86: *Sincere Appreciation and Loss of Friendship*. One of the most outrageous human characteristics involves being mysteriously rejected by a close friend who has been sincerely appreciated. The severity of friendship loss is directly proportional to the level of appreciation. It only occurs to certain individuals and began occurring shortly after the disappearance of the Fluorite peace keeping crystal over 2,500 years ago. Another deviously designed quantum energy system is the cause for the unpleasant phenomenon, wrecking many friendships for thousands of years into the future.

Robert comments how horrible that is, and Morris comments that that's one of the worst things, how a quantum energy system just cannot stand truly good friendships, and are designed to destroy them!

Next, they view plate number 75: *Memories Stored on Location*, which talks about the fact that many memories are triggered in people when they visit certain locations. While some people think memories are stored in the brain, the truth is, many memories are stored in the ethereal energy field around each person and that memories are also stored on location, literally recorded within the matter of the material items of any location, such as the rocks, soil, trees, or even buildings.

They talk about it and realize that's how psychics read information from knives and other artifacts. They read the information recorded in the matter of the artifact itself.

They view yet another plate: *Energy Field Absorption and Character Repetitions*, plate number 89. When two friends spend time together, their energy fields and character traits become absorbed into each other, and they can feel each other's characteristics for hours or sometimes days after they've separated from each other. What happens is that their energy fields become impressed upon each other and become synchronized as they interact with each other. This is the result of a positive energy system which is designed to cause people to achieve better friendships with each other.

Fraxino comments that that's more like it, a positive outlook on friendships. They comment on the plates for a while longer, turn off the crystal base computer, and go into the kitchen.

Glecko and Sosta feed them all breakfast. Then they, except Rinto, drive 100 kilometers south to search for more artifacts in the ancient galactic dump site. They stop and fill up with hydrogen fuel at an Exxoll station on the way.

Once at the dump site, Rudy finds an egg-shaped crystal, this one with a Sycamore (*Platanus*) seedball cluster image within.

Then they find a second bronze crate, this one containing 144 bronze plates with hieroglyphic writing on them, while other plates have square pieces of crystals impregnated into them. Plus, there is a corner compartment of various colors of crystals, most of them greenish-yellow.

Rudy picks up an orange one and suddenly experiences a rush of thoughts telepathically being given to him, along with Morris feeling a rush of thoughts, as well. Suddenly Rudy knows English, quite to everyone's surprise. Sudden language acquisition. Earlier, Glecko had learned English, and Chispo had learned Spanish.

After that surprise, they carry the heavy bronze crate to the vehicle-craft and return to Zantaayer, where they examine the contents on Rinto and Fraxino's crystal base computer. The bronze plates are a bunch of data keys or programming plates for a mission that is soon to come their way, Morris feels.

They view one more holographic plate: *Linkage of Souls and Friendship*, plate number 90, which talks about how friendship is a very important trait for soul advancement, and as many souls interact and learn together in the world of the spirits, they on higher levels can plan their lives together, causing synchronicities and coincidences to happen to their physical counterparts on Earth so they can meet each other and become the friends they are destined to be.

They comment on that plate, and then they drive to Zantaayer's Myrtillo Cinema to see *Vision from the Ciruclar.*

Chapter 2: THE ALASKA PROJECT PROPOSAL

All of them watch the movie, *Vision From the Ciruclar.* A man named Quinoteh has a vision about Zantaayer's first settlers from Atlantis. He leads an expedition to the Ciruclar Mountains, where they dig and find a bronze crate of rocks and crystals. One of them is a rare sacred story stone, and as Quinoteh telepathically reads it, he extracts a story of a quest for galactic communication and soul travel between various races of different star systems. They view Cresma welcoming the Atlantean colonists, and then Quinoteh makes efforts to re-establish contact with their ancient homeland of Atlantis.

Chispo, Rinto and Fraxino quietly translate to the others to keep them filled in. They laugh for what they actually know, because several weeks ago, they had actually found one of those sacred story stones in the galactic dump site. It revealed the origin of the *Liriodendron*, the Tulip Poplar or Flowering Sun Tree.

They talk about the movie and its meaning on the way back to the Zapatero's home.

That night, Rudy sneaks into the room where Rinto and Fraxino have their crystal base computer. There he takes the lid off the second bronze crate. As he reaches for another crystal, Fraxino arrives just in time, wrenches him away from the crate, and wrestles him to the floor. The others arrive and scold Rudy, telling him those crystals are likely dangerous, that not all Atlantean artifacts are benign. Rudy finally gets off his high horse, realizes his mistake, and they return to bed.

At breakfast the next morning, Glecko announces that *Kellogg's* has just expanded to a galactic level, and he hands them a box of *Kellogg's* Bran Flakes Esperaña. Everybody is surprised that the cereal box has totally Earth's alphabet. Robert realizes it has no BHT, and Glecko proudly says, "That's right." He goes on to explain that he was a chemist and that Butylated Hydroxytoluene is a dangerous byproduct of production that has no business ever being placed in foods and that it is strictly prohibited on their world of Artenia, and *Kellogg's* knows it. All hazardous chemicals are flown *straight* to Al Nitak, a far better incinerator than what their planet could produce.

Morris realizes there are no TV's or radios, and Chispo explains that there aren't any because transmission of electromagnetic waves is prohibited on Artenia, to respect other intelligent races who are sensitive on their world. All of Astrelcom's long distance phone communication is done by trunk cables and fiber optics.

Tom, the galactic salesman, suddenly arrives, and he announces the major project in mind. They drive up to the rim of the Ciruclar Mountains where Tom officially presents the plans of the major galactic switching station in northeastern Alaska's mountains. Tom reveals his true name, *Tomarius*.

The station will involve literally millions of Earth's telephone numbers, the numbers being made available over a 15 year period, during which time many new area codes will be added to the telephone systems of the United States, Canada, Great Britain, and other participating countries, all under contract and agreement with Galactic Federation rules and guidelines. Hidden charges will appear on all phone bills near the time of completion to pay for the costs.

Everyone is amazed, and Tom also tells about the time frozen bodies. He offers them US $33,000 cash if they can revive the bodies. They accept the project enthusiastically, and Tom transmits them the visual image of the three mountains in Alaska. With that, they agree to meet there in two days, and Tom teleports away.

They get back in their vehicle-craft, and they drive to Rinto and Fraxino's secret cave. They are impressed by their crystal room and lab. Then they return down the mountain to Zantaayer, arrive home, and Rinto and Fraxino prepare two briefcases of crystals to take with them.

They climb back in the craft and take off flying to southern Zotola, specifically to visit Orolizo and the Atascosa people. Orolizo might be an important link in the project.

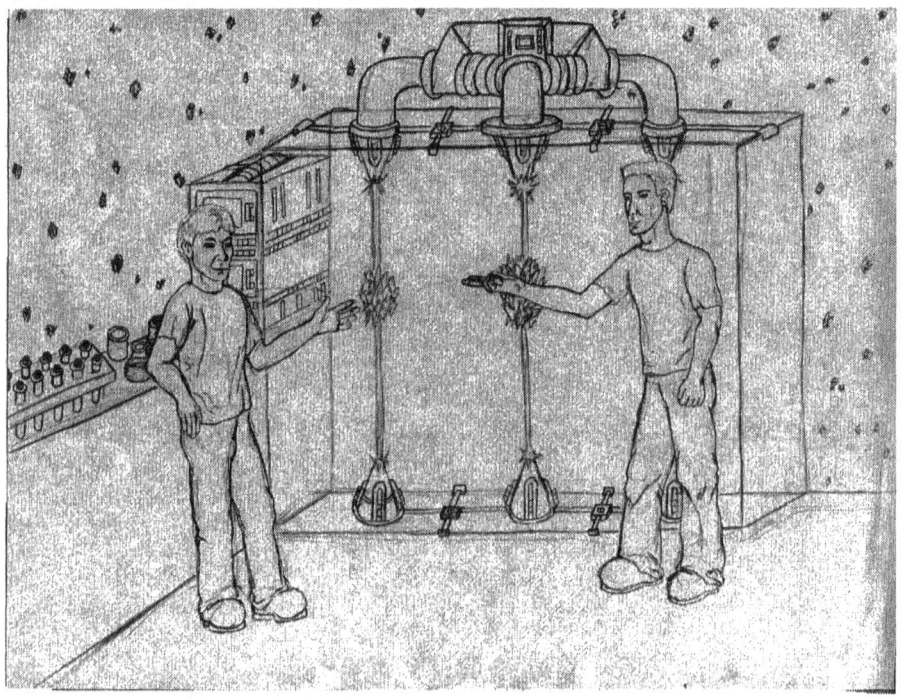

Chapter 3: THE ATASCOSA LINK

In less than three hours, they reach the Cloerinne Mountains where the Atascosa people live in one of its remote, inaccessible valleys. A river called the Makeeseldruff River runs through it, and while Chispo fills them in on the people there and tells other tall tales, Rinto lands in a meadow beside the river.

The Atascosa people are a rare race, their ancestors having been direct descendants of the original humans of Artenia 72 million years ago. Their skin has a touch of green, a genetic trait left over from bygone days many millions of years ago when some of the genetic characteristics of trees were combined with the genes of some of the humans, to utilize photosynthesis and survive possible food shortages.

Zocanto, the Atascosa leader, sees them arrive, and he and his people greet them as they step down from their craft. They are glad to see each other. Orolizo arrives and welcomes them all to his house where he and his sister Lumela live.

Chispo, who had hit it off really well with Orolizo during their previous visit, fills Orolizo in on Mexico, all the projects they had done, and how things went with Pegaso, Orolizo's soul link in Mexico. Orolizo is amazed by all they have done.

Chispo casually mentions *Vision from the Ciruclar* and the sacred story stone, and that they had also found one in the galactic dump site. Orolizo is amazed and reveals that he has one, having found it in a cave of the Cloerinne Mountains some years ago. He shows it to everyone. This sacred story stone reveals the history of the deciduous fruit trees, that the original ancestor of the fruit trees is the *Celtis*, the Hackberry.

Morris is impressed and decides to lecture about an important subject: genetics, how present day Earth humans have hardly scraped the surface on genetics and have no idea of the serious repercussions of genetically modifying foods. He goes on about the origin of life on separate planets in other star systems, talks about how many tree species on Earth are of extraterrestrial origin, and finishes by talking about a major conspiracy among the scientific community and how centuries ago, they purposefully hid much of the ancient Atlantean data about the trees and their origins.

Lumela arrives home. Steven and Andrew momentarily turn on for her, until Morris redirects the energy flows and breaks the trance. Orolizo and Lumela decide to accompany the others to Alaska, and they take a walk along the Base Cliff Trail to enjoy the forest and cliffs along the valley's rim.

At night, Morris, Chispo, and the others identify several stars, and they sleep for the night at Orolizo and Lumela's house. Early in the morning they board Rinto and Fraxino's vehicle-craft and go visit the ancient paintings in northern Mexico prior to going to Alaska.

Chapter 4: ANOTHER VISIT TO CHIQUIHUITILLOS

They arrive at the double mesa and climb up to the cliff walls. They are impressed by them, and Morris suddenly feels tingling sensations when they arrive at the drawing of 37½ cross-hatched diamonds in 7 columns. Chispo and Robert had earlier realized a coincidence, and Morris now confirms that the drawings tell a story of the dolphins' old home world of Delikadove.

Morris is also impressed by the dolphin/whale image.

Rudy notices it and points out that it's also an image of a human face. Morris is even more impressed! It's an icon to say that dolphins, whales, and humans are of all one race! Morris tells Robert and Chispo about their links to the dolphins, says there's another one of them also linked, but doesn't tell that yet.

They observe the paintings for two hours then return to the vehicle-craft. Rudy and Morris argue about whether or not the Atlanteans used verbal speech. Morris insists that of course they did, and seeing that Rudy doesn't realize that, he's alleviated that Rudy didn't pick up extra knowledge when he touched that orange crystal.

Next, they fly up to the mountain ridge top on the way to Bustamante, and they observe the site where their deactivating device blew up the rocks. They talk for a while, then descend to Bustamante, soon arriving at Rudy's house. Morris talks about other level programming.

Bustamante has a population of around 3,000 residents, and most of them are lifetime natives. The whole town in some ways is like a large family with everyone connected to everyone else in some way. There are no banks, no law offices, no fast food restaurants, no convenience stores, and no traffic lights. There is not even a fuel station, the nearest one being a Pemex station ten kilometers away.

Bustamante is situated in a grove or oasis of mostly Pecan trees and is at the foot of the mountains, the main feature being the Lion's Head Mountain, locally called Cabeza de León, elevation 1,860 meters.

Roel, Rudy's brother, has just arrived home from Zacatecas, quite to everyone's surprise. They happily greet each other and they take Orolizo and Lumela over to Pegaso's house so they can meet him. Upon arriving, they greet each other, and Pegaso and Roel shake hands as friends again. Pegaso apologizes to Roel and Rudy for the firecracker incident.

Suddenly, Pegaso, Orolizo, and Lumela experience a telepathic force of energy, and they suddenly learn each other's languages! They are surprised and now start visiting, feeling a strong connection of friendship.

Some of them walk to the plaza. Andrew is suddenly attracted to a young muchacha named Perlona. They visit the Cantu's store and they laugh about a new sign, a joke. They visit Alvaro and later return to Rudy's house for the night.

The next morning, both Andrew and Chris back out of the project. Andrew wants to spend the summer in Bustamante . . . with Perlona. Chris simply returns to Tennessee. Rudy escorts Andrew to her house.

The others walk over to Pegaso's house. Orolizo and Lumela have hit it off so well with Pegaso and his sisters that they decide to stay with them. Never mind Alaska!

Robert gets worried about who will stay in on the project.

Morris reveals that Rudy is the other one who has a link to the dolphins. In a past life, Morris and Rudy were at odds.

They re-gather at Roel and Rudy's house. Both Roel and Rudy decide to stay home. Alaska is too cold, plus the mosquitoes! More than that, Rudy is annoyed by Morris' vast knowledge and abilities.

Six of them: Rinto, Fraxino, Chispo, Robert, Steven, and Morris, board the vehicle-craft, leave Bustamante, and teleport to Alaska.

Chapter 5: THE TIME FROZEN FINDINGS

They are now flying over northeastern Alaska. Fraxino steers the craft into a ravine tucked into the western slopes of Mt. Isto, the easternmost of the three mountains, the other two being Mt. Chamberlin and Mt. Michelson. They are tall mountains at nearly 3,000 meters.

They land near a grey building. Tom and his friend Caymar are already there, and they greet them. The grey building has just arrived, having been teleported in by the Sirians.

Everybody takes a look around. The scenery is phenomenal, glaciers, glacial lakes, waterfalls and streams of rushing water are prevalent everywhere.

Right away, they climb the ridge with Tom and Caymar, and they dig up the bronze crates. They can't find any more, but Morris feels sure there are more bronze crates, Robert transports himself to Mexico, fetches Roel, and returns with him. In minutes, Roel's locator instincts take over, and he finds three more crates along the ridge. They dig them up and, with difficulty, carry them down the ridge into the cove.

They open them up and observe the time frozen bodies. Steven notices the all-one-race icon on the clothing of one of the frozen bodies, and he's amazed!

Morris figures out how to revive them, and he teleports himself away, along with the crates, stays gone, and minutes later, they appear into existence again.

The lids of the five crates come off, and out climb their occupants alive and well. Triumph! Morris has revived them, having successfully awakened them from their time frozen sleep. There are 3 females and 2 males. What Morris did was use the help of an expert dolphin friend.

The 5 Atlanteans are so glad to have their lives back. They become oriented and begin speaking and quite to Rinto, Fraxino, and Chispo's surprise, they speak the same as Artenian. The 5 Atlanteans realize the scenery has changed a lot, and Fraxino tells them they were time trapped, for 12,500 Earth years. They react in surprise!

As the Atlanteans begin to explain what they were doing, Roel feels a sudden urge to go home. Robert transports him back to Mexico, then returns back to Alaska.

The Atlanteans tell their names: Latorna, Tecoloteh, Quicho, Seglima, and Chameur. They explain that they were making a device-craft for soul travel and their project room was in a cave deep within Mt. Isto, and its entrance is now buried under the ice of the glacier above them.

Tom and Caymar are very pleased the Atlanteans are revived, and according to his promise, he pays the group of them US $33,000 cash. They divide the money but give half of it to Morris since he did the reviving. Robert takes $4,000 of it to Roel since he found three of the five crates.

Robert soon returns to Alaska, tells them Roel was ecstatic to be paid that money. Rudy was a different story. He had turned his back to Robert while he was handing Roel the money. Roel, however, sent word that they are welcome anytime, and he was going to set Rudy *straight* about all of them.

Robert and Chispo realize the painful truth that good feelings and connections of friendship are still no guarantee of friendship. Rudy had taken a dislike to the group, and he had been scared off by Morris' phenomenal amount of knowledge.

They take a walk up the cove and glacier to search for the device-craft. On the way up, Tecoloteh explains the meaning behind the all-one-race icon, that it indeed represents dolphins, whales, and humans all combined, and how it is a clever derivation of illusionary graphics from their high technology. They also talk about sacred story stones.

Latorna relates the corruption of Atlantis' government 2,500 years prior to the disaster and how a very important Fluorite peace keeping crystal was stolen from their society at that time, which caused the corruption to begin.

Fraxino tells the Atlanteans that he knows that story, and he tells them they found a box of 144 holographic plates in a galactic dump site on their world. That really surprises the Atlanteans because they were the creators of those plates, Chameur being the main compiler of the data!

Everyone is amazed at how destiny can make the pieces of the puzzle fall in place so perfectly.

Quicho relates the story of how they were just ready to install the data into their device-craft from the plates as a means to eliminate the bad energies of planet Earth at that time, but they were apprehended by unscrupulous Atlantean government officials and were time frozen.

A fleet of 65,000 Atlantean had fled to Al Nitak, and 400 of the worse scientists and government officials were made to stay behind. A year later, Cresma Atenkor had sent another craft to take any remaining survivors to Al Nitak. Cresma's last name was Atenkor.

The 5 Atlanteans amaze Rinto, Fraxino, and Chispo again when they tell them that they knew Cresma personally and were friends of his!

Latorna brings up that they had a second bronze crate with 144 data plates, and Fraxino tells them that they had just found a second crate in that galactic dump site only days ago. A joyous smile comes across the faces of the Atlanteans. They jump with joy and give thanks for the amazing synchronicity! Even Morris is surprised, and he explains that people who achieve the right level of thinking can brings events to a junction at exactly the right moments and cause wonderful events to blossom forth. They can time things right. That's how destiny works.

Latorna further explains that the main purpose of their device-craft project was for soul travel and for time travel, to give the victims of Atlantean society the chance to ascend and leave the bad energies behind. Plus, they were going to release good energies to circulate around the world and eradicate the bad energies.

They are around halfway up the glacier by now, and the Atlanteans determine that the entrance to their project room is under all the ice of the glacier, and that it was likely covered soon after the disaster. A blessing in disguise, Chameur points out. They explain more reasons.

Suddenly, a large spacecraft arrives in the cove. It is from Sirius B and contains Tom and Caymar's crew from the Galactic Federation. At least 20 Sirians step out of the craft. Tom teleports himself up to the glacier and talks to the others about the location of the entrance. They decide to penetrate the ice instead of melt it away, since it is so large.

The crew members re-enter the spacecraft, and it flies up to the glacier and lands on top of it. They begin excavating a tunnel 5 meters wide and 4 meters high. The Atlanteans guide the way, and the Sirian crew has various types of digging equipment and other machinery to take out the rubble.

Two Atlanteans, Latorna and Quicho, stay with Tom and the crew. Rinto stays with them and translates while the other 3 Atlanteans and the others go with Caymar to the grey building down in the cove.

Soon everyone is munching away on Sirian food, complete with live grains and prana.

Chispo tells Tecoloteh and the other Atlanteans what stories were on the sacred story stones. Chameur agrees that the origin of the *Liriodendron* is true and accurate, and she reveals more names and details. They briefly talk about the *Celtis* tree, and Chameur goes on to tell how trees spin in their own level of reality, that they bring in an untuned world with them. Chameur has, more than the others, an uncanny sense of the spirit world.

They talk about the egg-shaped tree cone crystals that were also found at the galactic dump site, and Chameur tells quite a story about the significance of the stars and rings on the egg-shaped Pine cone crystal.

The Atlanteans tell that they lived at what was then a latitude of 45° south in the northern part of Atlantis and directly south of what is now South America. They are from a small town called Atenkor, which is also where Cresma is from. There was a coastal metropolis nearby called Ennohoness, which until 2,500 years before, used to be called Texclozantess as far back as records went. Mountains were beautiful and forested with Southern Beech trees, Fern Trees, and other exotic plants, trees, and heaths. There was a decent amount of technology. However, there was no air pollution.

They continue chatting about various subjects and about the holographic plates. Tom and his crew work on the excavating several more hours and come in later to get some sleep.

Chapter 6: DEVICE-CRAFT UNDER THE GLACIER

It is now July 27, 1985.

Tom and his crew continue excavating the horizontal tunnel. They are making good progress, already having penetrated 100 meters into the glacier. They estimate another 50 meters to go. Some of the Atlanteans are overseeing the operation. Morris, Robert and Steven, along with Chispo, Rinto and Fraxino spend some time observing and also help in carrying bucketloads of ice and rubble out of the tunnel.

One of the Sirian crew members, Dotsero, announces that he sees rock. They wet the ice, shine a light beam through the ice, and locate the entrance under still 10 meters more of ice and 20-25 meters further ahead. They start up their machines and excavate up to it, after which they use flame throwers, instead of excavating with machinery.

The rocky entrance is plugged with 12 meters of ice, but they continue melting their way through it. Breakthrough is made with joyous triumph.

The Atlanteans enter with apprehension and walk the 200 meters to their research room, wondering if their device-craft is still there. It is indeed, and they exclaim with joy!

It is quite a sight to see with its colors of gold and green with reflective rainbow colors. It is approximately 2½ meters in width, 2 meters high, and 7 meters long. Similar to Rinto and Fraxino's cruiser craft, it was grown over a period of several months using a mixture of silicon and other strong and durable metals such as Vanadium. Tom and Caymar are impressed beyond words as they marvel over a piece of technology over 12,000 years old. The others are impressed, as well.

Chameur meditates and telepathically opens the device-craft's door, and to their relief, everything is there and intact inside. The apprehenders had been unsuccessful in unlocking the door. Only the two bronze crates had been taken from beside the device-craft.

Suddenly, everyone hears moaning and cracking sounds, but that's from the shifting ice of the glacier above. Tom suddenly realizes the need to reinforce the tunnel and sends his crew and spacecraft home for their Titanium-Vanadium Expansion Reinforcing Kit.

A 3D holographic movie begins to play, just outside the device craft, showing the whole apprehending procedure, including what had become of the bronze crates.

As the apprehenders arrived, Chameur managed to telepathically lock the door to the device-craft. The four apprehenders used crystals and disarmed the Atlanteans, removing them from the cave and into their flying vessel, where they placed each one of them in a time frozen bronze crate, after which they haphazardly buried them on the ridge above.

Next, they took the two bronze crates out of the cave, flew to Antarctica, and handed the two crates to the crew of the last escaping spacecraft of Atlanteans. They lied and said there were only two Atlanteans and that they were time frozen and here they were. The apprehenders attempted to return to Alaska, but met their doom, crashing into the mountains of South America. Good riddance!

Cresma was unaware of the scandal. His genuine request had fallen into corrupt hands. The spacecraft flew to Al Nitak, and it arrived seconds later, landing on the Ciruclar Mountains above Zantaayer. The hurried spacecraft crew quickly delivered the two crates to Cresma who questioned them about the three others, but the spacecraft crew hadn't the time to discuss it and had to leave! Cresma was taken aback, but was much more so when he and a specialist later opened the crates down in Zantaayer and discovered holographic plates instead of two of his friends!

In panic, Cresma ordered the crates to be carefully buried a good 100 kilometers away from Zantaayer, and also ordered a mass dumping of all precious rocks and crystals and other sacred items. They wanted to maintain their peace and harmony at all cost.

Once Cresma buried the bronze crates, telepathic contact was lost, and the 3D holographic movie ends.

Everyone is really taken by the movie. Morris explains how senseless that mass dumping was, that if Cresma had just stopped and thought about it instead of panicking, he would have realized the supreme value of what was dumped.

Rinto, Fraxino, and Chispo are shocked at Cresma's actions. Everyone is. Fraxino admits that the mass dumping is not told in any of Artenia's history books. Morris comments that all of them have gathered as a means of destiny, to restore the song or historical truth. Even Cresma's senseless actions were meant to happen that way, as a means to cause them to gather and solve this problem. Everyone is impressed by Morris' insight.

With that, Morris announces it's time to return to the world of the dolphins, and he gives one more important piece of information which might ease the project's completion, that the existence of the subconscious mind is a myth, a learned response which gives humans the excuse of committing unacceptable actions. The human mind can become unified and the conscious and subconscious can merge into one program.

Morris brings on the energy of the pink glow and whirring wind, and he vanishes, with sparks of silver and white energy! The others are surprised beyond belief . . . that Morris was a dolphin in disguise all the time! They contemplate and analyze their whole friendship with Morris, and how he was such a diversified being.

Tom and the crew return in the spacecraft with the reinforcing kit, and they line the entire inside of the tunnel in three to four hours, using a special chemical process.

They decide to penetrate beyond the project room and excavate a large room under the mountain for the large galactic switching station, which is to everyone's approval. They move the Atlanteans' device-craft to the side of the project room to protect it better.

The next day, they penetrate another 200 meters and then begin excavating the big room, using laser cutters to slice out the rock sections. Tom estimates a week of work. They also discuss the installation of entrance doors to keep out intruders. They arrive at a combination of 1013068750.

They talk with Tom about Morris' strange disappearance when he transported himself away last night. Tom already knew about it and comments that Morris is a very diversified being who is aware of other levels, along with his vast amount of alien knowledge. Tom and Caymar then walk up the glacier to begin work.

Fraxino invites everyone else to Zotola. They decide to go, but Quicho and Seglima stay, to watch their device-craft. They still don't trust Tom and his crew.

Chameur, Latorna, and Tecoloteh convince Quicho and Seglima that Tom and Caymar are genuine and honest.

The others pack their belongings in their backpacks, and they board Rinto and Fraxino's Velosa cruiser craft parked 100 meters away from the grey building. The Atlanteans are impressed by it and with Rinto and Fraxino's abilities. They explain how it drives and flies.

Quicho and Seglima come to collect the five time frozen crates, to take them up to the project room. They wish the others well on their trip to Zotola. Using the crystal power of the Ulexite main controls crystal, Rinto causes the craft to leave the ground, accelerate swiftly to the north, after which a green glow envelopes them and they disappear.

Chapter 7: RETRIEVAL OF THE TWO CRATES

They are now flying over the desert valley in Zotola heading north toward the Ciruclar Mountains. Al Nitak is low in the western sky, as it is nearly the end of the day.

Chameur and the other Atlanteans are impressed with emotion at the beauty of planet Artenia. Using hydrogen instead of fossil fuels, there is no air pollution.

Fraxino plays *The Hydragyros* in their on-board holodisk player.

Rinto makes a thrilling landing on the tree-lined gravel road along the rim of the Ciruclar Mountains. Chameur comments how wonderful the Southern Beech trees are, and she tells them the Atlantean name for them: Noirtrel Alaktt. Chispo then says in Artenian they are called Nortralakt Trees. Atlanteans enjoyed them when going on retreats to the mountains of Antarctica.

They descend the winding gravel road into Zantaayer, soon arriving at the Zapatero's house. They step outside, experience 98% Earth's gravity and realize the change in technological styles of the houses. Tecoloteh explains that back in Atlantis, they used to grow their homes, not too different from Tom's tunnel lining process.

They greet Glecko and Sosta who welcome them inside. Glecko recognizes who Chameur, Latorna and Tecoloteh are when he sees the all-one-race icon on their clothing, that they are Atlanteans! Rinto and Fraxino explain how they found them and revived them.

They enter the house and tell Glecko all about it. Sosta has already left to another part of the house. Glecko admits he knows about the all-one-race icon, which surprises his sons. One of Glecko's teachers taught it in ancient history.

Tecoloteh explains the whole history of that icon.

They decide to see the movie, *Vision from the Ciruclar.*

Before going to the movie, they eat supper, and then they go into Rinto and Fraxino's computer room. The Atlanteans are overjoyed to see their two bronze crates and to find all of the holographic plates still intact.

Rinto turns on the computer setup, and they view several plates, including plate number 7, *Medicinal Herbs and Plants of Atlantis*, and they view a small flowering plant, Quanac (*Quastris illustris*). They are impressed at how well Rinto and Fraxino's computer setup works. Chameur explains quite a bit more about the Quanac. It was used for treating stomach aches and pains, which were prevalent throughout Atlantis.

They then go to the movie and get some laughs for what they knew to really be true.

That night, Robert has a dream about the Fluorite peace keeping crystal that was stolen from Atlantis, and he realizes the crystal he and his friends found on planet Aleyone in the Pleiades is the same one spoken about in the holographic plates! He tells the others the next morning, and everyone is amazed they hadn't realized it earlier.

The Atlanteans definitely want to see that crystal, now atop Mt. Timpanogos in Utah.

While Rinto and Fraxino copy all of the holographic plate data into their computer setup, Chispo takes the others on a trip to Zantaayer's central library and other places for several hours. They visit the University of Zotola, and the beach as well. Chispo and Chameur begin to take to each other.

Meanwhile, Rinto and Fraxino talk with Tecoloteh who stayed with them. He tells them more about the compartment of crystals, how dangerous they are, and how lucky Rudy was to have been prevented from touching any more of them. Rinto copies all of the data to a backup cube of Ulexite.

The others return, and they pack to leave. They take the two bronze crates with them. Chispo stores the backup Ulexite cube at his house. They all board the vehicle-craft. Fraxino drives them to the crest of the Ciruclar Mountains, where they leave the ground, swiftly accelerate, and return to Earth's Alaska.

Chapter 8: THE EXOTIC PEACE KEEPING CRYSTAL

They fly south toward the 3 mountain peaks, and come in for a landing on the glacier near the tunnel entrance. Tom and his crew have already excavated quite a bit, and there is a large pile of rocks on the glacier already.

One of the Sirian vehicles emerges from the tunnel and carries Rinto, Fraxino, and the others, including their two bronze crates, into the tunnel and to the project room. Quicho and Seglima are glad to see everyone, want to know all about Artenia's Zotola and are overjoyed to have their two bronze crates back. They're really surprised to learn that the Fluorite peace keeping crystal is back on Earth, and on Mt. Timpanogos.

All of them board Rinto and Fraxino's craft, and they fly down to Utah to see the crystal and record the peace keeping qualities for their device-craft.

Chispo and Chameur sit by each other and take even more of a liking, perhaps *love*, for each other. Chameur is the available one of the five Atlanteans, and Chispo fits the bill very well.

Tom and his crew have been excavating the big room, at first in a rectangular cubical design, but changed the design to pyramidal at the suggestion of the Atlanteans. Quicho and Seglima relate the details of that design change to the others.

The Atlanteans also tell the others more about Atlantis, and planet Earth in those days, that Atlantis was the main center of world trade and commerce, but there were newer settlements, Atlantean colonies, in Earth's northern hemisphere. Atlantis had galactic trade, as well.

They talk about levitation technology, those who stayed behind after the disaster, and talk about other hidden records in high mountain tunnels and caves of other continents.

As they fly south at 2,500 km/h, they observe the Canadian Rockies, Montana, Yellowstone NP, and then they descend, to come in for a landing on the steep slopes of Mt. Timpanogos in Utah.

Rinto causes the craft to hover, while Robert and Steven locate the appropriate cliff ledge, after which they carefully land on its narrow surface, the most inaccessible ledge of them all. There are Fir trees, grasses, and moss.

They carefully step down from the craft and look around. The ledge is some 200 meters above the alpine meadow directly below them. They make their way north along the narrow ledge, finding the crystal in good shape. It is egg shaped, colored green, and it measures 25 cm from end to end. Within it is an orange pyramidal shaped piece of Citrine ingeniously grown within it. The five Archaeopteris seedlings are still there, alive and well.

The Atlanteans marvel over the crystal, and they record the necessary peace keeping qualities from it. They are amazed at its self illumination qualities, as well.

Robert explains how they found the crystal on planet Aleyone, the puzzle presented to them, and the hints given to them telepathically by some Archaeopteris trees. Since the crystal was way up on a ledge where they found it and since the trees on the ledge were Archaeopteris trees, they had brought five seedlings to plant around the crystal at its new location on Mt. Timpanogos.

Chameur commends their wise choice to plant Archaeopteris seedlings here and says the tree will later be discovered by the people of Earth and be realized with equal regard as the Ginkgo.

Rinto and Fraxino decide to definitely record the peace keeping crystal's energies, for the Atlantis history project. Fraxino runs back to the craft for a Kanágran crystal and a Calcite one, as well.

Chameur relates the origin of the Archaeopteris, that they called it Irquiarluz, and that it came from a star 120,000 light years away and called Plenidi. The planet was Tuepeic, which was dying of volcanic gases. 370 million years ago, they were brought to Earth, to flourish for 25 million years, after which they were teleported away, all of them, and returned to Tuepeic, which by then had recovered.

Fraxino returns from the craft, and they record the peace keeping data.

They observe the beautiful scenery, talk some more, then return to the craft. Rinto drives and they carefully lift off, after which they swiftly accelerate upward and to the north, soon achieving a speed of 2,500 km/h and a cruising altitude of 30,000 meters.

Several hours later, they arrive back in Alaska and land on the glacier. Tom is outside and greets them. They tell him what's happened and bring him up to date. Tom acknowledges the remarkable characteristics of the peace keeping crystal.

They enter the tunnel. Tom walks on toward the big room while Quicho and Seglima load the data of the crystal into the device-craft's central computer. Their next project is to program it with all the data tablets and holographic plates from the two bronze crates, a process that will take two days. Quicho and Seglima were the experts at programming. Latorna was more the leader of the whole project. Tecoloteh had been the gatherer of the materials, and Chameur had been the expert in compiling the stories onto the holographic plates.

Tom and Caymar emerge from the big room. They have further plans. Tom explains that they need a large Ulexite cube, of similar high quality as that which Rinto and Fraxino use in their vehicle-craft. It needs to be 20 cubic meters! Galactic Federation suppliers have Ulexite, but Rinto and Fraxino's piece is much purer. They talk it over and decide to obtain it from a mine in southern Zotola.

Tom also talks about the methods that will be used to get the millions of phone lines up to Alaska, and he reveals the real reason for the construction of the Alaska pipeline. Tom then teleports to the federation for the money.

Rinto, Fraxino, and Chispo talk over plans on how to obtain such a large piece of Ulexite, complications involved, whether Tom and his crew would have to laser cut it out of the quarry, etc.

Tom appears with 1,200 Zotolan zúbolas in hand and gives it to them as payment for the Ulexite slab. Tom and Caymar make plans for their crew to arrive in their spacecraft several hours later.

Robert and Steven are sort of put off by Rinto and Fraxino because they ask them not to come with them this time. It is suggested they go visit Chris and Richard Bell in the Planet of the Islands.

Tom and Caymar come along with Rinto, Fraxino, Chispo, Chameur, Latorna, and Tecoloteh. They close the door, and the craft leaves without Robert and Steven! They wonder if they ever contributed to Rinto and Fraxino. Yes, they definitely did, for knowing where that Fluorite peace keeping crystal was.

They transport away to the Planet of the Islands.

Chapter 9: SEPARATE PROJECTS AND ADVENTURES

Robert and Steven make their appearance in the grand arboretum owned by Chris and Richard's family. Early in the summer, Tom had helped Chris and Richard install a thousand-line step office, having teleported it away from

Kingston Park, Georgia.

They walk to the large concrete building housing the Earth museum. Chris and Richard greet them, glad to see them, and they catch up with each other. Richard asks where the rest of them have gone. Robert and Steven answer that they went their separate ways. Some had to work. Others got tired of it, and others fell in love and stayed behind.

Robert and Steven tell about their adventures to Sirius, Vega, and the Pleiades, and how they searched for and found a lost ancient crystal stolen from Atlantis. They relate their adventures to Al Nitak with Rinto, Fraxino, and Chispo, their adventures in Mexico, and that they are now working on a huge galactic switching station in Alaska.

Chris and Richard have been connecting customers to their step office, and they've been travelling to different star systems, collecting more trees for their arboretum. They show them some of their new trees, and also some 20-meter tall Archaeopteris trees.

Then they transport away to Alaska to see the galactic station.

*   *   *

The craft makes its appearance over the Zuehl Sea, south of Zotola. Rinto is driving. They come down for a landing on a highway and drive to Milvilona Canyon where the Ulexite mine is. They arrive right as the owner is closing the

77

gate. They pull up beside him, speak with him, and talk him into selling the 20 cubic meter slab of Ulexite, offering him 1,200 zúbolas as payment. Though he had been hesitant, he perks up at the offer and says yes.

The man whose name is Ocotiyo reopens the gate, and they drive up to the mine, actually quarry. They introduce themselves, talk it over, and make arrangements for Tom's crew to come with the spacecraft, quarry the piece, and leave, to be out of there by no later than 4 AM, when his next group of workers arrive. He also asks them to keep it quiet, so neighbors won't freak out.

Ocotiyo is surprised but glad to meet Tom and Caymar, and the Atlanteans. He assures everyone he is okay with beings from other worlds, and says that two or three times a year strange people arrive wanting Ulexite for special uses, such as astral travel, space communication, etc.

Tom telepathically sends for his crew and spacecraft. Ocotiyo wishes them well and drives home for the night.

In minutes, the spacecraft appears over the quarry, floats over to the gravel parking area, and lands. Several vehicles exit through the hatch below, descend into the quarry, and they use special laser cutters to cut the slab out of the bedrock. Next, they levitate the piece upward and into the craft, followed by the vehicles. The hatch closes, and the spacecraft becomes airborne, attains 50 meters in altitude, and teleports back to Alaska.

Tom and Caymar briefly accompany them to Alaska to oversee the arrival of the Ulexite slab, after which they pop over to Rinto and Fraxino's house in Zantaayer. Tom wants to discuss some supplement projects to do with soul travel and telepathy, and interfacing that into their phone lines.

Meanwhile, Rinto, Fraxino, and the others drive out of the mine, down to the coastal highway, and they fly to Zantaayer. They talk about Ulexite and how it was used in Atlantis.

When they descend into Zantaayer, Latorna remarks how it reminds her of Taltipocheh, one of Atlantis' cities.

Once they arrive, Chispo announces that he and Chameur are going up north to Caloma for several days. Rinto and Fraxino joke with Chispo about being in love.

*   *   *

Tom, Caymar, and their crew and spacecraft safely arrive in Alaska. Vehicles exit the spacecraft, along with the floating slab of Ulexite, which they guide into the tunnel. Tom commends Dotsero, one of the crew leaders, on the excellent job they did in quarrying the Ulexite. They decide to temporarily store the slab next to the Atlanteans' device-craft, to be moved into the big room once the excavating is finished.

Tom and Caymar finish overseeing the slab safely stored, and they walk back out onto the glacier to go visit Rinto and Fraxino. Caymar reminds Tom that they have yet to put up the security doors. Tom admits that it had slipped his mind. Tom re-enters the tunnel to direct Dotsero and his crew to take the spacecraft and fetch two doors from the Galactic Federation warehouses. They walk back out to the glacier. Dotsero and his crew board the spacecraft and fly away, cresting Mt. Isto on the way.

Tom and Caymar then teleport themselves to Zantaayer. It is night. Rinto and Fraxino haven't arrived yet, so Tom and Caymar walk the rim road of the Ciruclar Mountains, enjoying the forest of Southern Beech trees. They comment on how remarkably clear the air is on planet Artenia.

As they walk, they talk over the plans they have for Rinto and Fraxino. They also compliment Morris and his remarkable talents, how he revived those five time frozen Atlanteans, his association with dolphins, etc.

After an hour, they teleport to the Zapatero's backyard.

*   *   *

Rinto and Fraxino have just arrived. Chispo and Chameur have already crossed the backyards to his house. Rinto looks into the backyard, wondering about Tom and Caymar, and he witnesses them making their appearance.

Tom paces back and forth as he and Caymar explain the project plans, including soul travel experiences and telepathic communication through the phone lines. They want to interface those features with personal computers, and by the new millennium, many of Earth's residents will have computers with access to dialable services, many of which will be secretly routed through the galactic station. Government official hotlines and other high ranking officer lines will be connected to the station, as well. Information storage and retrieval will also be available.

Tom then informs them of the *Internet*, a system of dialable receivers to give Earth's residents better access to information and to help abolish intelligence suppression conspiracies. They want to establish open galactic trade and abolish the secrecy that is prevalent on Earth.

Plus, they want to interface virtual time travel experiences.

All of the above has the motive of boosting the consciousness of the people of Earth to an awakening to meet galactic level standards.

They also want visitors to the station to have access to various machines or devices for first-hand experiences. Tom explains that they need special storage crystals to be intelligently grown, and crystal arrays to achieve the above said goals. He offers Rinto and Fraxino 100,000 zúbolas to grow the appropriate crystals and arrays.

With enthusiasm, they shake hands on the deal. Tom and Caymar teleport back to Alaska. Rinto and Fraxino tell Latorna and Tecoloteh all of what Tom and Caymar said.

They all enter the house and get some sleep. The next morning, Glecko has breakfast for everyone. He gives his sons some positive encouragement on the project they are about to begin.

They talk about some of Earth's intelligence suppression conspiracies, and Glecko tells them he knows about Sodium Fluoride, how it's worm geared into public drinking water, and how a check for $50,000 was written to the American

79

Dental Association so they would promote Sodium Fluoride and say that it's good for cavity prevention. However, the truth is, Sodium Fluoride dulls intelligence.

On Artenia, Sodium Fluoride and other byproducts are flown *straight* to Al Nitak and properly disposed of.

Glecko goes on to talk about lead, expressing his disapproval of how it is added to Earth's gasolines, that it has no business ever being put into automobile fuels!

Special interest groups and other factions control a lot of Earth's scandals. Glecko encourages his sons to grow their project crystals accordingly, to help squelch and abolish all of those scandals!

Rinto and Fraxino confidently assure their father they will. They go up into the attic to sort through their crystals and rocks. They carry three full boxes to their vehicle-craft. They gather other flasks, tools, and supplies and drive up to their secret cave in the mountains.

Chapter 10: CHISPO AND CHAMEUR

Chispo and Chameur walk across the backyards to Chispo's house where they sleep for the night. His parents are away as usual.

An hour before the crack of dawn, Chispo gets up, rounds up some extra clothes for Chameur from his mother's closet. He takes the Ulexite cube over to the Zapateros and puts it in the vehicle-craft, returns, and he and Chameur leave for Caloma in Chispo's Velva Dibe car.

After crossing Zantaayer, Chispo fills up with hydrogen fuel at an Exxoll station. He complains about the increase in the price, now at 12 duocibols per liter.

100 kilometers into the trip, they stop and take a walk along the beach. After that, the highway turns inland. Chispo drives all day, as it's a long drive. They listen to Zotolan pop music in the on-board holodisk player. They talk about many things, including Atlantean music.

By early afternoon, they reach Caloma, which is greener and not so desertlike as Zotola. After several more hours of driving, they crest the Urlachia Mountains. At Chameur's flirtatious urging, they park and take a walk along the mountainous rim trail called the Wyndham Way. Al Nitak is just setting in the northwest sky, and the lights of the city of Zwever can be seen way below through the trees.

They enjoy the walk, swapping tall tales, and Chameur realizes how similar Chispo is to her past lover Qwintelo of Taltipocheh in Atlantis. Before they totally realize it, they embrace and kiss each other affectionately.

They return to his car, and he drives them down the mountainous road into Zwever and to his Aunt Esalina's house. Views are great from her house. Zwever is more of a city of mountains, the city itself at an average of 1,650 meters above sea level and the surrounding mountain peaks reaching up to 3,800 meters. The city has a population of 65,000, and through its center runs the Vovvitlet River.

Esalina happily greets Chispo and his Atlantean friend Chameur. Isn't Esalina surprised to find out Chameur is from Atlantis, from the past, and *really* surprised to find out that Chameur was a good friend of Cresma Atenkor! They talk about Atlantis, about what happened to the other fellows Chispo brought with him several weeks earlier, and Esalina tells them about Cliss and his new job, over in Eastern Caloma.

Cliss is studying rare and exotic plants from Atlantis, which certainly perks up the interest of Chispo and Chameur. Chispo calls him on the phone, and he says he knows of the Quanac plant. They decide to drive there the next day.

They stay at Esalina's for the night, and the next morning Esalina wishes them well. Chispo drives Chameur to Zwever's central market, then on to Echelosa, 400 kilometers to the east. Echelosa is a small town situated on a plateau forested with Southern Beech trees and Pine trees. They find Cliss' house, and he happily greets them and welcomes them inside.

Cliss happens to have the afternoon off, so they take an afternoon hike to the small spring where the Quanac flowers grow. Chameur collects four of them, two for Rinto and Fraxino's project with the other Atlanteans, and the other two for planet Earth. They hike back to Echelosa, where they call Rinto and Fraxino. They fly their vehicle-craft up to see them, collect the Quanac plants, and take them back to Zantaayer, to include their peace giving qualities into their crystal growing

81

project.

Chispo and Chameur spend the night with Cliss. They take a cruise around Echelosa that night. Cliss introduces them to several of his friends, and they swap stories.

The next morning, Cliss has to go to work. Chispo and Chameur take a road trip in the Velva Dibe. They fill up at an Exxoll station and continue further east and then north to a town called Davino. On the way, they stop by a riverside and take a swim, where they splash and play like children.

At Davino, Chispo inquires about hiking and camping in the mountains. From Davino, the highway climbs into the Tarima district, a scenic mountainous area with Pines and Cypresses. They park at the narrow crest, and hike a ridge for several hours, to arrive at a beautiful alpine lake and meadow. They camp under some Fir trees.

They explore the area, take another swim, and they enjoy the exquisite scenery.

They talk, and Chameur relates a story about the Ginkgo and how Atlantean scientists brainstormed and literally brought the extinct tree back into existence, snatching a forest of them from the past and bridging it with the present, to begin their lives as the new Ginkgo on planet Earth.

They also talk about the Sycamore or Buttonball Tree being of extraterrestrial origin.

Chispo relates how the seed ball cluster has importance for keeping peace and harmony among the races, that it would be a good mascot tree for all the races.

Chameur is impressed with Chispo's explanation, and they go on to talk about Alquzoque, a legendary man from the sea, a man from a different dimension of reality. He was highly respected and regarded as a guardian of the sea. He could change himself and come onto land and he passed on many sacred and valuable stories to the Atlanteans.

Chispo and Chameur gaze into each other's eyes. Love feelings turn on. Hormones flare up, and in short order, they start kissing. The make for the tent where they go all out and make love, bringing on that special heat and feelings of ecstasy.

They sleep peacefully together, *so* peacefully!

The next day they explore the region, enjoying their time together and their peaceful friendship. They know they want to spend the rest of their lives together as partners. They camp again under the Fir trees.

The next day, clouds move in, and they hike back to the car. Chispo drives the rest of the day on their trip back to Zantaayer. They arrive at sunset. They had been away six days.

When they arrive home, Chispo's mother, Vironga, is there. She greets them and says she noticed some of her clothes missing. Chispo explains, and Vironga understands. She and Chameur talk a while, and the three of them go inside to visit some more.

Later than night, Chispo and Chameur go next door and inquire about Rinto and Fraxino. They are still up in the mountains with the other Atlanteans, and they hope to have everything finished by morning.

Chapter 11: STRANGE DISCOVERY AT THE STATION

Meanwhile, Tom and Caymar and their crew have been busy excavating. They have made serious progress on their excavating of the big room. Upon completion, the room will be in the shape of a giant 4-sided pyramid, 50 by 50 meters in area, with the apex being 42 meters high.

Robert, Steven, Chris and Richard are presently working inside one of the huge Galactic Federation warehouses under one of the many deserts of Sirius B. They are busy soldering wire contacts of the huge main central device, a cube measuring 25 meters on each side. Contacts number in the millions.

A crew of Sirians is also working on the structure.

Suddenly all of the Sirians cry out as if in pain. Something's wrong with Tom, Caymar, and their crew in Alaska! Robert, Steven, Chris and Richard, and several Sirians teleport to Alaska. Upon arriving, they find several Sirian crew members running from the tunnel in fear. Tom, upon leaving, intercepts Robert, Steven, Chris and Richard, and he tells them there's been an accident, that a shaft of rock dislodged and killed three crew members: Denchulo, Huante, and Llacudo.

They are in grief. Some crew members work to clear the rubble and free the bodies, but they are crushed beyond recovery. Work stops immediately. Funeral arrangements are made.

The funeral takes place on Sirius B's southern Guaitecoh Mountains, forested with tall and graceful Kanofleh trees. The climate is warm and sunny, and Wasser, chief of the Sirian Council, performs the funeral ceremony.

After the 30-hour mourning period, Tom and Caymar and their crew return to Alaska to finish the excavating. Dotsero leads the crew as they clean up the rest of the fallen rubble.

To their surprise, they find a Lyran bronze tablet 30 by 40 centimeters in size. It had fallen with the shaft of rock. They examine the foreign script. Tom and Caymar stare at it in amazement. It turns out to be a dedication plaque for the colonists of Atlantis, having come from Vega. It also designates this mountain as the location for galactic communication, and it asks for peace and harmony always.

Tom, Caymar, and the crew become more curious. They hoist themselves up to the shaft near the apex, climb up into it and discover a chamber room of various crystals, a requiem, measuring 7 by 9 meters in size. At the far end is a 1 x 1 x 1.5 meter block of orange Calcite.

Suddenly, a 3D holographic movie projects itself above the block. It is a recording of Morris as an old man. The scene is on the shoreline of an alien world of purple seas and skies. Morris greets those who enter and talks about this requiem room he mysteriously created in the 200,000 year ago past!

The 3D movie plays a second time. Tom, Caymar, and several crew members are baffled. They climb back down the shaft, cancel the last bit of apex excavating, and they fetch from the spacecraft and bring in their Titanium Vanadium Expansion Reinforcing Kit to line the big room, before any more rocks fall down.

When they re-enter the room, ready to line its walls with the special resin, there stands Morris . . . along with Denchulo, Huante, and Llacudo, alive and perfectly intact! Tom and everyone are so surprised and in disbelief. Morris tells them he realized the casualties, and he took appropriate action to rescue them from the dead, by performing a time jump and reviving them. He snatched a duplicate of each one right before the accident and therefore was able to restore them.

Tom, Caymar, and the others commend Morris on his brilliance.

He says he was glad he could do it. He explains about his requiem, about the Lyran bronze tablet, and that his galactic name is Maalkarrai. Morris transports away, returning to the dolphins.

They are very grateful to Morris. Now Tom and Caymar no longer have to go before the Galactic Federation and explain. The three dead crew members are restored and are back alive and well.

While Tom, Denchulo, Huante, and Llacudo teleport to Sirius B to give Wasser the good news, Caymar, Dotsero, and other crew members line the walls of the pyramid room. They install a staircase to access the requiem room above.

Tom returns, commends the lining process, and next they teleport in the large pieces of equipment from the warehouse on Sirius B. They still have to bury a fiberoptic cable to the west to access the Alaska pipeline. They also have a stone lodge to build, and towers to install on the ridge above.

Tom, Caymar, and Dotsero teleport to the big underground warehouse on Sirius B to prepare the teleportation procedure to Alaska. Tom and his crew place a special forcefield on the huge pieces and they disappear, to arrive seconds later in Alaska.

Chapter 12: PROJECT CRYSTALS FROM ZOTOLA

Tom and Caymar and their crew are successful with teleporting the equipment.

Rinto, Fraxino, Latorna and Tecoloteh have been very busy growing the crystals for the special use devices in the galactic station. Chispo and Chameur have been out of the way of the others for six days, travelling to Caloma.

On a crisp sunny morning, Rinto and Fraxino and the others return from the mountains. Chispo and Chameur returned the night before. Fraxino greets Chispo asking how his honeymoon went. They joke around a bit.

They have grown several large crystal setups and arrays. One piece is in the back of the vehicle-craft. Three larger ones are still in the cave.

Chispo and Chameur remark that Rinto, Fraxino, and the Atlanteans *have* been busy on their project. Chispo is impressed, declaring, "Far out!"

Rinto describes the features of the crystal setup with them and that it's going directly under the large Ulexite slab. Latorna tells them that another setup is for time travel, another is for the station's main frame central, and that another one is for blocking intelligence suppression.

They enter the house. Glecko and Sosta are just getting up. Glecko comes outside to see the crystal array they brought down with them. He is impressed and compliments them on the fine work and their triumph. Sosta tells them she's proud of them, too.

They go inside for breakfast. Glecko reads Zantaayer's morning newspaper and exclaims about another scandal from planet Earth. This one's about MSG (Monosodium Glutamate), talking about how food and drug companies have been paid under the table to approve the nasty chemical for enhancing food flavor. Clever cover-up names are used to disguise it. Intelligence suppression is the main driving force behind it. MSG has no business ever being added to food products!

Glecko reminds them that nasty chemical products are flown *straight* to Al Nitak, a far better incinerator than what Artenia has to offer. Why can't Earth capture that bright idea?

They finish breakfast, board the vehicle-craft, and head back to Alaska. They have the Quanac flowers on board, too.

It is August 5, 1985. Upon arriving, they notice that the sending/receiving towers are in place on the ridge. They are already building the stone lodge. Rinto, Fraxino, Tecoloteh and Latorna carry the crystal assembly through the tunnel to the pyramid room.

Tom marvels over it. Quicho and Seglima completed the programming in two days. Chispo is amazed at the fast work of Tom, Caymar, and their crew. Most of the equipment is already installed. The large cube main frame central is in place, along with other special use machines to the right.

They levitate the 4 by 5 meter Ulexite slab into the room and cradle it into place. Then Rinto, Fraxino, Tecoloteh and Latorna place the newly grown crystal assembly in a special place beneath the cradle.

Fraxino informs Tom that there are three more pieces too large to carry and that they are still in their cave. Tom suggests using the spacecraft, but that would be too cumbersome. Rinto suggests Tom coming with them and using teleportation. Tom agrees, tells Dotsero to man the crew, and they walk out to the glacier.

Tom, Caymar, Rinto, Fraxino, Chispo and Chameur fly in the vehicle-craft to Zantaayer. They appear over the Ciruclar Mountains and come in for a fast landing on the gravel road, whizzing by trees and startling Tom and Caymar. In minutes, they reach the roadside above the gully, where they walk the 20 minutes down to the cave entrance.

Caymar tells them the whole story about the death of the three Sirian crew members, their marvelous revival by Morris, the bronze Lyran tablet, and he tells them all about the mysterious requiem room above the pyramid room.

When they reach Rinto and Fraxino's project room inside the cave, Rinto explains the use of each crystal array. Tom commends their fine work, especially that of Latorna and Tecoloteh.

Tom proceeds to teleport each of the three pieces one at a time. He moves his walking staff, and each one disappears, after which Tom teleports to Earth's Alaska to receive them.

Rinto asks his brother why they struggled getting that other crystal assembly out of there the hard way!

They spend a while looking around, return to the vehicle-craft and fly back to Earth's Alaska.

Upon arriving on the glacier, Robert, Steven, Chris and Richard transport in, making their appearance. They greet each other and catch up with each other on what they've been doing.

Chispo boasts about the four crystal masterpieces his friends have grown. The Atlanteans are installing the time travel crystal array into their device craft.

Another array is placed inside the main frame central cube, and the other one is installed into a top secret government soul travel device.

Chispo notices the spiral stairway to the apex, and they go check out Morris' requiem room. They marvel at the Lyran tablet, then climb up the shaft, watch the 3D movie clip of Morris, marvel at the room and crystals, and descend the staircase.

Rinto, Fraxino, Robert, Chispo, Chameur, and Steven return to the glacier, board the vehicle craft, and fly to British Columbia to find a deep moist virgin forest to plant the Quanac flowers. They choose a remote lake region of Vancouver Island. Chameur and Chispo take the flowers and plant them. Rinto and Fraxino wait in the craft.

They camp for the night by the lakeshore.

The next day, they fly back to Alaska. Upon arriving, Tom and Caymar greet them, and they commend them on all the work they've done.

They still lack installing the fiberoptic cable to the west, and completing the stone lodge.

As Rinto, Fraxino, and the Atlanteans have successfully accomplished a job well done, Tom takes them into his spacecraft where he rewards them the 100,000 zúbolas. He opens a silver container and hands them the stack of notes. He will be paying Robert, Steven, Chris and Richard separately for their work. They all thank Tom for the money, and they divide it appropriately among themselves.

Tom tells everyone to come back a week from now. Everything will be up and running by then.

Rinto offers Robert and Steven to come to Zotola with them. Robert accepts, but Steven declines. Rinto says he didn't mean to brush them off last week. It's just their project at hand was so intense. Steven says he understands, not to worry about it.

The Atlanteans aren't sure, but they believe they'll want to live in Zantaayer. The five of them, and Robert, decide to go with Rinto, Fraxino, and Chispo back to Zantaayer.

Quicho and Seglima need two more hours to finish programming the device-craft. Meanwhile Robert and the others take a walk around the facilities, exploring the glacier and cove below. Sirian crew vehicles are laser cutting a trench for the fiberoptic cable. Work is progressing on the lodge.

Robert notices that the galactic station will be ready long before the new millennium, but perhaps it might take another 15 years to free up all those millions of phone numbers and add new area codes in a subtle way without suspicion.

Steven, Chris and Richard stay and work another week. Tom walks over to Robert, knowing he's going to Artenia with Rinto, Fraxino, and the others. He pays Robert $500 for the work he has done.

When Quicho and Seglima finish the programming, Robert and the Atlanteans board the vehicle-craft with Rinto, Fraxino, and Chispo. They take off, arriving in Zotola in seconds.

They are now flying over the desert valley south of Zantaayer. Chispo plays the holodisk of *The Hydragyros*. So impressive the music is. Chispo says the group is predicted to soar to number one on Zotola's pop charts.

They land at the southern crest of the Ciruclar Mountains and descend on the highway into Zantaayer.

Twenty minutes later, they are arriving at the Zapateros. Glecko is just arriving in his Tolejo sedan. Rinto and Fraxino tell their father the station is built and all arrived safely. Their father commends them.

That night, they go see *The Hydragyros* live in concert at Zantaayer's University of Zotola, an excellent performance. Chameur predicts that the equivalent of *The Hydragyros* will exist on Earth in another 12 years.

For the next week, they tour Zantaayer, the central library, the beach, the Ciruclar Mountains, the galactic dump site, and they enjoy the beauty of the area.

They also make serious progress on their Atlantean history compilation. The Atlanteans are a great help. It turns out being 1,000 pages. They title it: *The Heritage of Atlantis*. They pay a printer 2,000 zúbolas to print 1,000 copies in Artenian and 250 copies in English. Rinto and Fraxino's history professor is really going to raise his eyebrows when he sees it.

Upon completion of that, they return back to Alaska, taking the 250 English version books with them.

The date is August 16, 1985. They land on the glacier, walk into the tunnel, and as they enter the pyramid room, Tom is just lifting up the lever, turning on the station. Perfect timing.

The lodge is all finished down in the cove, and the president and prime minister are presently staying there. They've been attending a secret summit conference in Fairbanks.

Mr. Mayfield is there, and Robert talks with him for a while.

There is a soul travel device. Chispo and Chameur are the first ones to use it. They take an astral travel trip to Atlantis, such an authentic experience, as if they really went there. Tecoloteh and Latorna astral travel to the Southern Beech trees and learn all about the extraterrestrial origin of that tree species. Next, Quicho and Seglima take a trip, astral travelling to a distant star system. They learn about the *Ficus sycomorus*, about Yom Kippur, and about the day of forgiveness.

The president and Britain's prime minister walk in with their armed body guards. Tom welcomes them, but quickly orders the guards to leave! No weapons nor ammunition allowed, strict Galactic Federation mandate! The guards reluctantly leave, and Tom, Caymar, and Dotsero give the two high officials a grand tour of the facilities.

When that tour is finished, they return to the lodge in the cove.

The first block of Earth's phone numbers has just been freed up. New York City has just added area code 718, freeing up many 212 prefixes. They have been beamed up to Alaska, and Caymar moves a big lever upward, bringing the numbers to life.

Chispo is the first one to use the station's phone system. He calls and surprises his cousin Cliss in Echelosa, Caloma. Tom calls Manta at the telephone station on Sirius B.

While more calls are made, Robert gives Steven a copy of *The Heritage of Atlantis*.

Tom declares the station a grand success! Many more blocks of phone numbers and many star systems will be added over the next 15 years, along with other special devices, plus a special experience apparatus from Delikadove, where Morris is. Morris has yet to reveal those details, but the dolphins are working on it.

The Atlanteans have their device-craft ready for time travel. They break the news that their device-craft can also fly, just like Rinto and Fraxino's vehicle-craft. They load the five bronze crates, to take to Cresma.

They say goodbye to Robert, Steven, and the others. Robert unloads his 250 books and Tom helps him teleport them to the step office building in Tennessee. Robert transports himself home, arriving in the corner of the woods. Tom and Caymar are already there, and they store the boxes of books inside the building.

They say goodbye to each other. Tom and Caymar teleport away and Robert uncovers his Ford LTD station wagon in the barn and drives it down to his house. Tomorrow, he will go visit Chris and Richard on the Planet of the Islands.

Meanwhile, the Atlanteans levitate their device-craft, fly out of the tunnel, and together with Rinto and Fraxino's craft, they fly away and teleport to Zantaayer. They disappear over Mt. Isto in a green flash.

EPILOGUE

The galactic station grows over the next 15 years. Government officials from all over the world visit from time to time. Spacecrafts and navess from other stars and galactic civilizations visit on regular basis, tending to business and connecting their star systems to the galactic station. It becomes a place of data storage, including *Internet* access and millions of dialable phone lines.

Long distance carriers levy a "Carrier Line Charge: and "Universal Connectivity Charge" on phone bills, to fund the station's progress. Even satellites are placed in orbit to accommodate calls. A masterpiece of its time, the galactic station would become a central pivot of communication and peace.

*   *   *

Rinto, Fraxino, Chispo and the Atlanteans arrive safely in Zantaayer. Hidden in the Ciruclar Mountains, they travel back in time 10,130 Artenian years, float over the grassy Ciruclar Mountains, and arrive in a much smaller Zantaayer.

They visit Cresma. Tears come to his eyes when he sees them. They tell him everything, show him the 3D holographic movie, and prevent the mass dumping of precious crystals that Cresma had planned to carry out the following week. They still go through with it, but make copies to be dumped instead. The original artifacts are safely stored in a museum.

The Atlanteans also give Cresma a copy of *The Heritage of Atlantis*.

Chispo and Chameur get married. Cresma conducts the ceremony. They decide to live in modern Zantaayer and live part of the time in old Zantaayer, as well.

Zotola's news media is spellbound when they receive an anonymous copy of *The Heritage of Atlantis*. A ten-page story about the book comes out in Zantaayer's newspaper. Newspapers throughout the region also report it. It is the talk of the town for months, until Rinto, Fraxino, Chispo and Chameur come forth and perform a formal launch of the book. Cresma comes forward in time and does the honors of the opening speech.

They do very well, enjoy travels and adventure, and become authorities in their fields.

*   *   *

Robert and his friends go back to their normal lives, attend their senior year of high school, and they all do well. Morris stays on Delikadove and without ever telling, he sends a holographic copy of himself to Earth to attend the rest of high school and live on Earth. In telepathic contact, he writes a book on dolphins and their origins.

Robert and his friends would have reunions from time to time, to take trips, and to visit their friends in Zantaayer.

The Atlanteans have placed a specially grown peace crystal way up high in the mountains of Antarctica. Over time, Earth would become a more peaceful place. Positive energies would prevail more and more.

Copies of:
>   1)*Mission of the Galactic Salesman*, ISBN: 1-886371-35-0 or 1-928798-04-7
>   2)*Mission Beyond the Ice Cave: Atlantis-Mexico-Zotola*, ISBN: 1-928798-00-4
>   3)*Heritage Findings from Atlantis*, ISBN: 1-928798-01-2

are available directly from the author at Armstrong Valley Publishing Company. They may also be ordered at retail price directly from Ingram Book Company of LaVergne, Tennessee.

ORDER FORM

Please send me:	quantity	amount
Mission of the Galactic Salesman		
special reduced price @$10.00	_____	$_____
Mission Beyond the Ice Cave:		
Atlantis-Mexico-Zotola @$15.95	_____	$_____
Heritage Findings from Atlantis		
@$15.95	_____	$_____
subtotal		$_____

Tennessee residents add 9.75% sales tax to subtotal
Plus shipping and handling for one book
    (surface rates: $3.00 within USA, $6.00 foreign)
Plus shipping and handling for each additional book
    (surface rates: $2.00 within USA, $4.00 foreign)   _____ $_____

Please remit funds in US dollars.   Total enclosed $_____
Make checks or money orders payable to the author: **Robert S. Sanders, Jr.**
Discounts:
10 to 99 books: 10% off
100 or more books: 20% off

Books make great gifts for your friends and relatives.

Send order to:
    Name_____
    Address_____
    City_____State_____Postal Code_____
Phone number (optional)_____

www.ingramcontent.com/pod-product-compliance
Lightning Source LLC
Chambersburg PA
CBHW031856170626
46807CB00004B/1755